VOICES FOR THE CURE

VOICES FOR THE CURE

A SPECULATIVE FICTION ANTHOLOGY
TO BENEFIT
THE AMERICAN DIABETES ASSOCIATION

EDITED BY
JAMES PALMER

WHITE ROCKET BOOKS

VOICES FOR THE CURE: A SPECULATIVE FICTION ANTHOLOGY TO BENEFIT THE AMERICAN DIABETES ASSOCIATION

Cover Design and Layout by Keith Howell

Book Design by Van Allen Plexico for White Rocket Books

A White Rocket Book
www.whiterocketbooks.com

ISBN 978-0-6151-8727-3

This book is set in Garamond and Arial typefaces.

First White Rocket Books Edition: January 2008

0 9 8 7 6 5 4 3 2 1

Acknowledgements

I could not have hoped to put something like this together without the help of so many kind and generous people.

To the authors: for your heartfelt enthusiasm, for giving me your best, for contacting me out of the blue and offering a story, I want to say thank you.

To Davey Beauchamp, whose own work showed me that this could be done, and told me how to pull it off.

To my friend Fox Gradin, for doing such a great job with the cover art.

To Keith Howell, for answering my call for cover layout help, and for doing such an excellent job. Keith would like to dedicate his work on the cover to his friends Darlene and Jean.

And last but certainly not least, to Kelley, my Muse, my soul mate, and the inspiration for this anthology. For all of your enduring love and support, and for just plain putting up with me, I give my unending love.

Contents

The Hand You're Dealt

Robert J. Sawyer

And ye shall know the truth, and the truth shall make you free—John 8:32

"Got a new case for you," said my boss, Raymond Chen. "Homicide."

My heart started pounding. Mendelia habitat is supposed to be a utopia. Murder is almost unheard of here.

Chen was fat—never exercised, loved rich foods. He knew his lifestyle would take decades off his life, but, hey, that was his choice. "Somebody offed a soothsayer, over in Wheel Four," he said, wheezing slightly. "Baranski's on the scene now."

My eyebrows went up. A dead soothsayer? This could be very interesting indeed.

I took my pocket forensic scanner and exited The Cop Shop. That was its real name—no taxes in Mendelia, after all. You needed a cop, you hired one. In this case, Chen had said, we were being paid by the Soothsayers' Guild. That meant we could run up as big a bill as necessary—the SG was stinking rich. One of the few laws in Mendelia was that everyone had to use soothsayers.

Mendelia consisted of five modules, each looking like a wagon wheel with spokes leading in to a central hub. The hubs were all joined together by a long axle, and separate travel tubes connected the outer edges of the wheels. The whole thing spun to simulate gravity out at the rims, and the travel tubes saved you having to go down to the zero-g of the axle to move from one wheel to the next.

The Cop Shop was in Wheel Two. All the wheel rims were hollow, with buildings growing up toward the axle from the outer interior wall. Plenty of open spaces in Mendelia—it wouldn't be much of a utopia without those. But our sky was a hologram, projected on the convex inner wall of the rim, above our heads. The Cop Shop's entrance was right by Wheel Two's transit loop, a series of maglev tracks along which robocabs ran. I hailed one, flashed my debit card at an unblinking eye, and the cab headed out. The Carling family, who owned the taxi concession, was one of the oldest and richest families in Mendelia.

The ride took fifteen minutes. Suzanne Baranski was waiting outside for me. She was a good cop, but too green to handle a homicide alone. Still, she'd get a big cut of the fee for being the original responding officer. After all, the cop who responds to a call never knows who, if anyone, is going to pick up the tab. When there *is* money to be had, first-responders get a disproportionate share.

I'd worked with Suze a couple of times before, and had even gone to see her play cello with the symphony once. Perfect example of what Mendelia's all about, that. Suze Baranski had blue-collar parents. They'd worked as welders on the building of Wheel Five; not the kind who'd normally send a daughter for music lessons. But just after she'd been born, their soothsayer had said that Suze had musical talent. Not enough to make a living at it—that's why she's a cop by day—but still sufficient that it would be a shame not to let her develop it.

"Hi, Toby," Suze said to me. She had short red hair and big green eyes, and, of course, was in plain clothes. You wanted a uniformed cop, you called our competitors, Spitpolish, Inc.

"Howdy, Suze," I said, walking toward her. She led me over to the door, which had been locked off in the open position. A holographic sign next to it proclaimed:

Skye Hissock
Soothsayer
Let Me Reveal Your Future!
Fully Qualified for Infant and Adult Readings

We stepped into a well-appointed lobby. The art was unusual for such an office—it was all original pen-and-ink political cartoons. There was Republic CEO Da Silva, her big nose exaggerated out of all proportion, and next to it, Axel Durmont, Earth's current president, half buried in legislation printouts and tape that doubtless would have been red had this been a color rendering. The artist's signature caught my eye, the name Skye with curving lines behind it that I realized were meant to represent clouds. Just like Suze, our decedent had varied talents.

"The body is in the inner private office," said Suze, leading the way. That door, too, was already open. She stepped in first, and I followed.

Skye Hissock's body sat in a chair behind his desk. His head had been blown clean off. A great carnation bloom of blood covered most of the wall behind him, and chunks of brain were plastered to the wall and the credenza behind the desk.

"Christ," I said. Some utopia.

Suze nodded. "Blaster, obviously," she said, sounding much more experienced in such matters than she really was. "Probably a gigawatt charge."

I began looking around the room. It was opulent; old Skye had obviously done well for himself. Suze was poking around, too. "Hey," she said, after a moment. I turned to look at her. She was climbing up on the credenza. The blast had knocked a small piece of sculpture off the wall—it lay in two pieces on the floor—and she was examining where it had been affixed. "Thought that's what it was," she said, nodding. "There's a hidden camera here."

My heart skipped a beat. "You don't suppose he got the whole thing on disk, do you?" I said, moving over to where she was. I gave her a hand getting down off the credenza, and we opened it up—a slightly difficult task; crusted blood had sealed its sliding doors. Inside was a dusty recorder unit. I turned to Skye's desk, and pushed the release switch to pop up his monitor plate. Suze pushed the recorder's playback button. As we'd suspected, the unit was designed to feed into the desk monitor.

The picture showed the reverse angle from behind Skye's desk. The door to the private office opened and in came a young man. He looked to be eighteen, meaning he was just the right age for the mandatory adult soothsaying. He had shoulder length dirty-blond hair, and was wearing a t-shirt imprinted with the logo of a popular meed. I shook my head. There hadn't been a good multimedia band since The Cassies, if you ask me.

"Hello, Dale," said what must have been Skye's voice. He spoke with deep, slightly nasal tones. "Thank you for coming in."

Okay, we had the guy's picture, and his first name, and the name of his favorite meed. Even if Dale's last name didn't turn up in Skye's appointment computer, we should have no trouble tracking him down.

"As you know," said Skye's recorded voice, "the law requires two soothsayings in each person's life. The first is done just after you're born, with one or both of your parents in attendance. At that time, the soothsayer only tells them things they'll need to know to get you through childhood. But when you turn eighteen, you, not your parents, become legally responsible for all your actions, and so it's time you heard everything. Now, do you want the good news or the bad news first?"

Here it comes, I thought. He told Dale something he didn't want to hear, the guy flipped, pulled out a blaster, and blew him away.

Dale swallowed. "The—the good, I guess."

"All right," said Skye. "First, you're a bright young man—not a genius, you understand, but brighter than average. Your IQ should run between 126 and 132. You are gifted musically. Did your parents tell you that? Good. I hope they encouraged you."

"They did," said Dale, nodding. "I've had piano lessons since I was four."

"Good, good. A crime to waste such raw talent. You also have a particular aptitude for mathematics. That's often paired with musical ability, of course, so no surprises there. Your visual memory is slightly better than average, although your ability to do rote memorization is slightly worse. You would make a good long-distance runner, but ..."

I motioned for Suze to hit the fast-forward button; it seemed like a typical soothsaying, although I'd review it in depth later, if need be. Poor Dale fidgeted up and down in quadruple speed for a time, then Suze released the button.

"Now," said Skye's voice, "the bad news." I made an impressed face at Suze; she'd stopped speeding along at precisely the right moment. "I'm afraid there's a lot of it. Nothing devastating, but still lots of little things. You will begin to lose your hair around your twenty-seventh birthday, and it will begin to gray by the time you're thirty-two. By the age of forty, you will be almost completely bald, and what's left at that point will be half brown and half gray.

"On a less frivolous note, you'll also be prone to gaining weight, starting at about age thirty-three—and you'll put on half a kilo a year for each of the following thirty years if you're not careful; by the time you're in your mid-fifties, that will pose a significant health hazard. You're also highly likely to develop adult-onset diabetes. Now, yes, that can be cured, but the cure is expensive, and you'll have to pay for it. So either keep your weight down, which will help stave off its onset, or start saving now for the operation ..."

I shrugged. Nothing worth killing a man over. Suze fast-forwarded the tape some more.

"—and that's it," concluded Skye. "You know now everything significant that's coded into your DNA. Use this information wisely, and you should have a long, happy, healthy life."

Dale thanked Skye, took a printout of the information he'd just heard, and left. The recording stopped. It *had* been too much to hope for. Whoever killed Skye Hissock had come in after young Dale had departed. He was still our obvious first suspect, but unless there was something awful in the parts of the genetic reading we'd fast-forwarded over, there didn't seem to be any motive for him to kill his soothsayer. And besides, this Dale had a high IQ, Skye had said. Only an idiot would think there was any sense in shooting the messenger.

After we'd finished watching the recording, I did an analysis of the actual blaster burn. No fun, that: standing over the open top of Skye's torso. Most of the blood vessels had been cauterized by the charge. Still, blasters were only manufactured in two places I knew of—Tokyo, on Earth, and New Monty. If the one used here had been made on New Monty, we'd be out of luck, but one of Earth's countless laws required all blasters to leave a characteristic EM signature, so they could be traced to their registered owners, and—

Good: it *was* an Earth-made blaster. I recorded the signature, then used my compad to relay it to The Cop Shop. If Raymond Chen could find some time between stuffing his face, he'd send an FTL message to Earth and check the pattern—assuming, of course, that the Jeffies don't scramble the message just for kicks. Meanwhile, I told Suze to go over Hissock's client list, while I started checking out his family. Fact is, even though it doesn't make much genetic sense, most people are killed by their own relatives.

Skye Hissock had been fifty-one. He'd been a soothsayer for twenty-three years, ever since finishing his Ph.D. in genetics. He was unmarried, and both his parents were long dead. But he did have a brother named Rodger. Rodger was married to Rebecca Connolly, and they had two children, Glen, who, like Dale in Skye's recording, had just turned eighteen, and Billy, who was eight.

There are no inheritance taxes in Mendelia, of course, so barring a will to the contrary, Hissock's estate would pass immediately to his brother. Normally, that'd be a good motive for murder, but Rodger Hissock and Rebecca Connolly were already quite rich: they owned a controlling interest in the company that operated Mendelia's atmosphere-recycling plant.

I decided to start my interviews with Rodger. Not only had brothers been killing each other since Cain wasted Abel, but the DNA-scanning lock on Skye's private inner office was programmed to recognize only four people—Skye himself; his office cleaner, who Suze was going to talk to; another soothsayer named Jennifer Halasz, who sometimes took Skye's patients for him when he was on vacation (and who had called in the murder, having stopped by apparently to meet Skye for coffee); and dear brother Rodger. Rodger lived in Wheel Four, and worked in One.

I took a cab over to his office. Unlike Skye, Rodger had a real flesh-and-blood receptionist. Most companies that did have human receptionists used middle-aged, businesslike people of either sex. Some guys got so rich that they didn't care what people thought; they hired beautiful blonde women whose busts had been surgically altered far beyond what any phenotype might provide. But Rodger's choice was different. His receptionist was a delicate young man with refined, almost feminine features. He was probably older than he looked; he looked fourteen.

"Detective Toby Korsakov," I said, flashing my ID. I didn't offer to shake hands—the boy looked like his would shatter if any pressure were applied. "I'd like to see Rodger Hissock."

"Do you have an appointment?" His voice was high, and there was just a trace of a lisp.

"No. But I'm sure Mr. Hissock will want to see me. It's important."

The boy looked very dubious, but he spoke into an intercom. "There's a cop here, Rodger. Says it's important."

There was a pause. "Send him in," said a loud voice. The boy nodded at me, and I walked through the heavy wooden door—mahogany, no doubt imported all the way from Earth.

I had thought Skye Hissock's office was well-appointed, but his brother's put it to shame. *Objets d'art* from a dozen worlds were tastefully displayed on crystal stands. The carpet was so thick I was sure my shoes would sink out of sight. I walked toward the desk. Rodger rose to greet me. He was a muscular man, thick-necked, with lots of black hair and pale gray eyes. We shook hands; his grip was a show of macho strength. "Hello," he said. He boomed out the word, clearly a man used to commanding everyone's attention. "What can I do for you?"

"Please sit down," I said. "My name is Toby Korsakov. I'm from The Cop Shop, working under a contract to the Soothsayers' Guild."

"My God," said Rodger. "Has something happened to Skye?"

Although it was an unpleasant duty, there was nothing more useful in a murder investigation than being there to tell a suspect about the death and seeing his reaction. Most guilty parties played dumb far too long, so the fact that Rodger had quickly made the obvious connection between the SG and his brother made me suspect him less, not more. Still ... "I'm sorry to be the bearer of bad news," I said, "but I'm afraid your brother is dead."

Rodger's eyes went wide. "What happened?"

"He was murdered."

"Murdered," repeated Rodger, as if he'd never heard the word before.

"That's right. I was wondering if you knew of anyone who'd want him dead?"

"How was he killed?" asked Rodger. I was irritated that this wasn't an answer to my question, and even more irritated that I'd have to explain it so soon. More than a few homicides had been solved by a suspect mentioning the nature of the crime in advance of him or her supposedly having learned the details. "He was shot at close range by a blaster."

"Oh," said Rodger. He slumped in his chair. "Skye dead." His head shook back and forth a little. When he looked up, his gray eyes were moist. Whether he was faking or not, I couldn't tell.

"I'm sorry," I said.

"Do you know who did it?"

"Not yet. We're tracing the blaster's EM signature. But there were no signs of forcible entry, and, well ..."

"Yes?"

"Well, there are only four people whose DNA would open the door to Skye's inner office."

Rodger nodded. "Me and Skye. Who else?"

"His cleaner, and another soothsayer."

"You're checking them out?"

"My associate is. She's also checking all the people Skye had appointments with recently—people he might have let in of his own volition." A pause. "Can I ask where you were this morning between ten and eleven?"

"Here."

"In your office?"

"That's right."

"Your receptionist can vouch for that?"

"Well ... no. No, he can't. He was out all morning. His sooth says he's got a facility for languages. I give him a half-day off every Wednesday to take French lessons."

"Did anyone call you while he was gone?"

Rodger spread his thick arms. "Oh, probably. But I never answer my own compad. Truth to tell, I like that half-day where I can't be reached. It lets me get an enormous amount of work done without being interrupted."

"So no one can verify your presence here?"

"Well, no ... no, I guess they can't. But, Crissakes, Detective, Skye was my *brother* ..."

"I'm not accusing you, Mr. Hissock—"

"Besides, if I'd taken a robocab over, there'd be a debit charge against my account."

"Unless you paid cash. Or unless you walked." You can walk down the travel tubes, although most people don't bother.

"You don't seriously believe—"

"I don't believe anything yet, Mr. Hissock." It was time to change the subject; he would be no use to me if he got too defensive. "Was your brother a good soothsayer?"

"Best there is. Hell, he read my own sooth when I turned eighteen." He saw my eyebrows go up. "Skye is nine years older than me; I figured, why not use him? He needed the business; he was just starting his practice at that point."

"Did Skye do the readings for your children, too?"

An odd hesitation. "Well, yeah, yeah, Skye did their infant readings, but Glen—that's my oldest; just turned 18—he decided to go somewhere else for his adult reading. Waste of money, if you ask me. Skye would've given him a discount."

My compad bleeped while I was in a cab. I turned it on.

"Yo, Toby." Raymond Chen's fat face appeared on the screen. "We got the registration information on that blaster signature."

"Yeah?"

Ray smiled. "Do the words 'open-and-shut case' mean anything to you? The blaster belongs to one Rodger Hissock. He bought it about eleven years ago."

I nodded and signed off. Since the lock accepted his DNA, rich little brother would have no trouble waltzing right into big brother's inner office, and exploding his head. Rodger had method and he had opportunity. Now all I needed was to find his motive. And for that, continuing to interview the family members might prove useful.

Eighteen-year-old Glen Hissock was studying engineering at Francis Crick University in Wheel Three. He was a dead ringer for his old man: built like a wrestler, with black hair and quicksilver eyes. But whereas father Rodger had a coarse, outgoing way about him—the crusher handshake, the loud voice—young Glen was withdrawn, soft-spoken, and nervous.

"I'm sorry about your uncle," I said, knowing that Rodger had already broken the news to his son.

Glen looked at the floor. "Me too."

"Did you like him?"

"He was okay."

"Just okay."

"Yeah."

"Where were you between ten and eleven this morning?"

"At home."

"Was anyone else there?"

"Nah. Mom and Dad were at work, and Billy—that's my little brother—was in school." He met my eyes for the first time. "Am I a suspect?"

He wasn't really. All the evidence seemed to point to his father. I shook my head in response to his question, then said, "I hear you had your sooth read recently."

"Yeah."

"But you didn't use your uncle."

"Nah."

"How come?"

A shrug. "Just felt funny, that's all. I picked a guy at random from the online directory."

"Any surprises in your sooth?"

The boy looked at me. "Sooth's private, man. I don't have to tell you that."

I nodded. "Sorry."

Two hundred years ago, in 2029, the Palo Alto Nanosystems Laboratory developed a molecular computer. You doubtless read about it in history class: during the Snow War, the U.S. used it to disassemble Bogatá atom by atom.

Sometimes, though, you *can* put the genie back in the bottle. Remember Hamasaki and DeJong, the two researchers at PANL who were shocked to see their work corrupted that way? They created and released the nano-Gorts—self-replicating microscopic machines that seek out and destroy molecular computers, so that nothing like Bogatá could ever happen again.

We've got PANL nano-Gorts here, of course. They're everywhere in Free Space. But we've got another kind of molecular guardian, too—inevitably, they were dubbed helix-Gorts. It's rumored the SG was responsible for them, but after a huge investigation, no indictments were ever brought. Helix-Gorts circumvent any attempt at artificial gene therapy. We can tell you everything that's written in your DNA, but we can't do a damned thing about it. Here, in Mendelia, you play the hand you're dealt.

My compad bleeped again. I switched it on. "Korsakov here."

Suze's face appeared on the screen. "Hi, Toby. I took a sample of Skye's DNA off to Rundstedt"—a soothsayer who did forensic work for us. "She's finished the reading."

"And?" I said.

Suze's green eyes blinked. "Nothing stood out. Skye wouldn't have been a compulsive gambler, or an addict, or inclined to steal another person's spouse—which eliminates several possible motives for his murder. In fact, Rundstedt says Skye would have had a severe aversion to confrontation." She sighed. "Just doesn't seem to be the kind of guy who'd end up in a situation where someone would want him dead."

I nodded. "Thanks, Suze. Any luck with Skye's clients?"

"I've gone through almost all the ones who'd had appointments in the last three days. So far, they all have solid alibis."

"Keep checking. I'm off to see Skye's sister-in-law, Rebecca Connolly. Talk to you later."

"Bye."

Sometimes I wonder if I'm in the right line of work. I know, I know—what a crazy thing to be thinking. I mean, my parents knew from my infant reading that I'd grow up to have an aptitude for puzzle-solving, plus superior powers of observation. They made sure I had every opportunity to fulfill my potentials, and when I had my sooth read for myself at eighteen, it was obvious that this would be a perfect job for me to pursue. And yet, still, I have my doubts. I just don't feel like a cop sometimes.

But a soothsaying can't be wrong: almost every human trait has a genetic basis—gullibility, mean-spiritedness, a goofy sense of humor, the urge to collect things, talents for various sports, every specific sexual predilection (according to my own sooth, my tastes ran to group sex with Asian women—so far, I'd yet to find an opportunity to test that empirically).

Of course, when Mendelia started up, we didn't yet know what each gene and gene combo did. Even today, the SG is still adding new interpretations to the list. Still, I sometimes wonder how people in other parts of Free Space get along without soothsayers—stumbling through life, looking for the right job; sometimes completely unaware of talents they possess; failing to know what specific things they should do to take care of their health. Oh, sure, you can get a genetic reading anywhere. Even down on Earth. But they're only mandatory here.

And my mandatory readings said I'd make a good cop. But, I have to admit, sometimes I'm not so sure.

Rebecca Connolly was at home when I got there. On Earth, a family with the kind of money the Hissock-Connolly union had would own a mansion. Space is at a premium aboard a habitat, but their living room *was* big enough that its floor showed a hint of curvature. The art on the walls included originals by both Grant Wood and Bob Eggleton. There was no doubt they were loaded—making it all the harder to believe they'd done in Uncle Skye for his money.

Rebecca Connolly was a gorgeous woman. According to the press reports I'd read, she was forty-four, but she looked twenty years younger. Gene therapy might be impossible here, but anyone who could afford it could have plastic surgery. Her hair was copper-colored, and her eyes an unnatural violet. "Hello, Detective Korsakov," she said. "My husband told me you were likely to stop by." She shook her head. "Poor Skye. Such a darling man."

I tilted my head. She was the first of Skye's relations to actually say something nice about him as a person—which, after all, could just be a clumsy attempt to deflect suspicion from her. "You knew Skye well?"

"No. To be honest, no. He and Rodger weren't that close. Funny thing, that. Skye used to come by the house frequently when we first got married—he was Rodger's best man, did he tell you that? But when Glen was born, well, he stopped coming around as much. I dunno. Maybe he didn't like kids; he never had any of his own. Anyway, he really hasn't been a big part of our lives for, oh, eighteen years now."

"But Rodger's DNA was accepted by Skye's lock."

"Oh, yes. Rodger owns the unit Skye has his current offices in."

"I hate to ask you this, but—"

"I'm on the Board of Directors of TenthGen Computing, Detective. We were having a shareholders' meeting this morning. Something like eight hundred people saw me there."

I asked more questions, but didn't get any closer to identifying Rodger Hissock's motive. And so I decided to cheat. As I said, sometimes I *do* wonder if I'm in the right kind of job. "Thanks for your help, Ms. Connolly. I don't want to take up any more of your time, but can I use your bathroom before I go?"

She smiled. "Of course. There's one down the hall, and one upstairs."

The upstairs one sounded more promising for my purposes. I went up to it, and the door closed behind me. I really did need to go, but first I pulled out my forensic scanner and started looking for specimens. Razors and combs were excellent places to find DNA samples; so were towels, if the user rubbed vigorously enough. Best of all, though, were toothbrushes. I scanned everything, but something was amiss. According to the scanner, there was DNA present from one woman—the XX chromosome pair made the gender clear. And there was DNA from one man. But *three* males lived in this house: father Rodger, elder son Glen, and younger son Billy.

Perhaps this bathroom was used only by the parents, in which case I'd blown it—I'd hardly get a chance to check out the other bathroom. But no. There were four sets of towels, four toothbrushes, and there, on the edge of the tub, a toy aquashuttle ... precisely the kind an eight-year-old boy would play with.

Curious. Four people obviously used this john, but only two had left any genetic traces. And that made no sense. I mean, sure, I hardly ever washed when I was eight like Billy, but no one can use a washroom day in and day out without leaving some DNA behind.

I relieved myself, the toilet autoflushed, and I went downstairs, thanked Ms. Connolly again, and left.

Like I said, I was cheating—making me wonder again whether I really was cut out for a career in law enforcement. Even though it was a violation of civil rights, I took the male DNA sample I'd found in the Hissock-Connolly bathroom to Dana Rundstedt, who read its sooth for me.

I was amazed by the results. If I hadn't cheated, I might never have figured it out. It was a damn-near perfect crime.

But it all fit, after seeing what was in the male DNA.

The fact that of the surviving Hissocks, only Rodger apparently had free access to Skye's inner office.

The fact that Rodger's blaster was the murder weapon.

The fact that there were apparently only two people using the bathroom.

The fact that Skye hated confrontation.

The fact that the Hissock-Connolly family had a lot of money they wanted to pass on to the next generation.

The fact that young Glen looked just like his dad, but was subdued and reserved.

The fact that Glen had gone to a different soothsayer.

The fact that Rodger's taste in receptionists was ... unusual.

The pieces all fit—that part of my sooth, at least, must have been read correctly; I *was* good at puzzling things out. But I was still amazed by how elegant it was.

Ray Chen would sort out the legalities; he was an expert at that kind of thing. He'd find a way to smooth over my unauthorized soothsaying before we brought this to trial.

I got in a cab and headed off to Wheel Three to confront the killer.

"Hold it right there," I said, coming down the long, gently curving corridor at Francis Crick. "You're under arrest."

Glen Hissock stopped dead in his tracks. "What for?"

I looked around, then drew Glen into an empty classroom. "For the murder of your uncle, Skye Hissock. Or should I say, for the murder of your brother? The semantics are a bit tricky."

"I don't know what you're talking about," said Glen, in that subdued, nervous voice of his.

I shook my head. Soothsayer Skye *had* deserved punishment, and his brother Rodger *was* guilty of a heinous crime—in fact, a crime Mendelian society considered every bit as bad as murder. But I couldn't let Glen get away with it. "I'm sorry for what happened to you," I said. The mental scars no doubt explained his sullen, withdrawn manner.

He glared at me. "Like that makes it better."

"When did it start?"

He was quiet for a time, then gave a little shrug, as if realizing there was no point in pretending any longer. "When I was twelve—as soon as I entered puberty. Not every night, you understand. But often enough." He paused, then: "How'd you figure it out?"

I decided to tell him the truth. "There are only two different sets of DNA in your house—one female, as you'd expect, and just one male."

Glen said nothing.

"I had the male DNA read. I was looking for a trait that might have provided a motive for your father. You know what I found."

Glen was still silent.

"When your dad's sooth was read just after birth, maybe his parents were told that he was sterile. Certainly the proof is there, in his DNA: an inability to produce viable sperm." I paused, remembering the details Rundstedt had explained to me. "But the soothsayer back then couldn't have known the effect of having the variant form of gene ABL-419d, with over a hundred T-A-T repeats. That variation's function hadn't been identified that long ago. But it *was* known by the time Rodger turned eighteen, by the time he went to see his big brother Skye, by the time Skye gave him his adult soothsaying." I paused. "But Uncle Skye hated confrontation, didn't he?"

Glen was motionless, a statue.

"And so Skye lied to your dad. Oh, he told him about his sterility, all right, but he figured there was no point in getting into an argument about what that variant gene meant."

Glen looked at the ground. When at last he did speak, his voice was bitter. "I had thought Dad knew. I confronted him—Christ sakes, Dad, if you knew you had a gene for incestuous pedophilia, why the hell didn't you seek counseling? Why the hell did you have kids?"

"But your father didn't know, did he?"

Glen shook his head. "That bastard Uncle Skye hadn't told him."

"In fairness," I said, "Skye probably figured that since your father couldn't have kids, the problem would never come up. But your dad made a lot of money, and wanted it to pass to an heir. And since he couldn't have an heir the normal way ..."

Glen's voice was full of disgust. "Since he couldn't have an heir the normal way, he had one made."

I looked the boy up and down. I'd never met a clone before. Glen really was the spitting image of the old man—a chip off the old block. But like any dynasty, the Hissock-Connolly clan wanted not just an heir, but an heir and a spare. Little Billy, ten years younger than Glen, was likewise an exact genetic duplicate of Rodger Hissock, produced from Rodger's DNA placed into one of Rebecca's eggs. All three Hissock males had indeed left DNA in that bathroom—exactly identical DNA.

"Have you always known you were a clone?" I asked.

Glen shook his head. "I only just found out. Before I went for my adult soothsaying, I wanted to see the report my parents had gotten when I was born. But none existed. My dad had decided to save some money. He didn't need a new report done, he figured; my sooth would be identical to his, after all. When I went to get my sooth read and found that *I* was sterile, well, it all fell into place in my mind."

"And so you took your father's blaster, and, since your DNA is the same as his ..."

Glen nodded slowly. His voice was low and bitter. "Dad never knew in advance what was wrong with him—never had a chance to get help. Uncle Skye never told him. Even after Dad had himself cloned, Skye never spoke up." He looked at me, fury in his cold gray eyes. "It doesn't work, dammit—our whole way of life doesn't work if a soothsayer doesn't tell the truth. You can't play the hand you're dealt if you don't know what cards you've got. Skye deserved to die."

"And you framed your dad for it. You wanted to punish him, too."

Glen shook his head. "You don't understand, man. You can't understand."

"Try me."

"I didn't want to punish Dad. I wanted to protect Billy. Dad can afford the best damn lawyer in Mendelia. Oh, he'll be found guilty, sure, but he won't get life. His lawyer will cut it down to the minimum mandatory sentence for murder, which is—"

"Ten years," I said, realization dawning. "In ten years, Billy will be an adult—and out of danger from Rodger."

Glen nodded once.

"But Rodger could have told the truth at any time—revealed that you were a clone of him. If he'd done that, he would have gotten off, and suspicion would have fallen on you. How did you know he wasn't going to speak up?"

Glen sounded a lot older than his eighteen years. "If Dad exposed me, I'd expose him. And the penalty for child molestation is also a minimum ten years, so he'd be doing the time anyway." He looked directly at me. "Except being a murderer gets you left alone in jail, and being a pedophile gets you wrecked up."

I nodded, led him outside, and hailed a robocab.

Mendelia *is* a great place to live, honest.

And, hell, I did solve the crime, didn't I? Meaning I *am* a good detective. So I guess *my* soothsayer didn't lie to me.

At least—at least I hope not ...

I had a sudden cold feeling that the SG would stop footing the bill long before this case could come to public trial.

The God Biz
A Miracle Brigade Story

Mike Resnick

Unless your name is Zeus or Jupiter or Jehovah or maybe Odin, take my advice and stay out of the God biz. It's no place for amateurs.

I could have told that to Max Enright, but of course he never asked. Well, not until after he'd already found it out the hard way.

Max was an exogeologist, which is to say, he was a geologist who specialized in alien worlds. He was pretty good at his trade. In fact, some say he was the best. He could find diamonds in asteroid belts after ten other exogeologists had explored them and swore there was nothing there but a bunch of little ugly rocks crammed together to make a few big ugly rocks. They say he could sniff out platinum from three systems away.

For awhile he worked for one of the huge cartels that was headquartered on Deluros VIII, and then another one that was based in the Spica system bought him off. Finally he sat down and did the math, realized that he was making about one credit for every 200 credits he earned for his employers, and decided to go independent. It wasn't that he needed the money; he'd already made enough to last him a lifetime. He was a bit greedy and a bit mendacious, but certainly no more so than normal. It was simply that he didn't know why 99.5% of the profits should go to a bunch of executives and shareholders who wouldn't know an Atrian moonstone from an Antarean singing pearl if it bit them (as Atrian moonstones are wont to do.)

Max did pretty well for himself at the outset. He went out to the Albion Cluster, found some awfully valuable things on a handful of worlds nobody had ever heard of, then went even farther toward the galactic core. Whenever he found an idyllic world (there were still a few left, kind of like New Tahiti but without all the resorts) he named it after himself, and made it all the way up to Max 8 before he remembered to name one for his mother. When he found a world with untapped riches (and there were a few of them, too), he'd stake a claim, and stick around long enough to set up a mining operation before moving on to the next world.

Still, what he liked best were not empty, unexplored worlds, but rather colony worlds, because no one was more interested in plundering a world of its riches than the people who lived there, and no one worked harder than those who had a stake in the outcome.

You could say that Max Enright Ltd. (that soon became his official name) was pretty pleased with himself and happy with his life, and you'd have been right.

Until the day he came to Socrates.

Of course, it wasn't called Socrates on the star charts or in the ship's navigational computer. It was Beta Scaparelli III, and was listed as uninhabited and unexplored.

His scanners told him his computer's information was wrong when he braked down to sub-light speeds a few million miles out.

It seems that there was metal on the planet. Not the kind you pull out of mines and melt down and purify. No, this was the kind of metal you find in a ship's hull, and a moment later his various sensing devices confirmed that there was indeed a ship on the surface. Or, to be more precise, the remains of a ship.

Beta Scaparelli III was an oxygen world, with 98.3% Standard gravity, and no harmful active or inert elements in the atmosphere. That made it possible, perhaps even likely, that the ship had been carrying a human crew. He drew closer to the planet, constantly magnifying images in his viewscreen, until he was finally able to make out the shape of the ship. It was definitely one of the Republic's, and finally he was able to read what was left of the identification on the hull: OCRAT 7.

He had his computer launch a search for a missing ship with the official name of OCRAT 7. There wasn't any. His next logical thought was that it had been DEMOCRAT 7, but there was no record of such a ship.

Then, because he was a cautious and thoughtful man, he ordered the computer to trace any missing ships with the letters OCRAT in their names. It looked, it hummed to itself, it looked some more, and finally it announced that it was going to have to access the Master Computer back on Deluros VIII at a rate of one thousand credits per hour or any portion thereof. Max gave his approval, and about three minutes later it found what it was looking for: it turned out that a colony ship identified as SOCRATES 72H had been reported missing and presumed lost 352 years ago.

So at least Max would be dealing with human beings. He was curious to see what kind of society they had formed, how it had evolved over the years, what new and undreamed-of inventions they'd come up with. He was sure they hadn't found the gold his instincts told him was here, or they'd long since have been exporting it, and the Republic would have known that the planet was inhabited.

He checked the computer to make sure that they'd be speaking Terran rather than the conglomerate of local languages that existed prior to the Republic's declaration that all Men would speak with one tongue, and was relieved to find out that that was indeed the case and he wouldn't have to use a translating device to speak to members of his own race.

He instructed his ship to seek out the nearest landing field, only to be informed that there weren't any. That was when he began to get the idea that maybe he was going to find a few less mind-boggling innovations and inventions that he had initially hoped for. (But on the plus side, it also meant that they wouldn't have the machines to find the gold he knew was there, or the tools to dig it out.)

He tried to radio ahead that he wanted to land and needed coordinates, only to learn that there were no radios on the planet. Or at least, not any functioning ones. He considered transferring to the ship's small landing shuttle, which could set down in a much smaller area, but the more he thought about it, the more he felt that he'd be much happier with his own galley and his own chemical shower, so he finally ordered the ship to land as close to the remains of the SOCRATES 72H as possible.

When it finally touched down Max unstrapped himself, killed the artificial gravity, bonded his pulse gun's holster to his right hip and his sonic pistol's to his left, opened the hatch, stepped out onto the small landing platform, and ordered the ship to lower the platform to the ground.

He looked around, and thought he saw some motion off to his left. He pivoted to confront whatever was there – and suddenly found himself facing a half-naked girl. Her figure was lean and willowy, her hair cascaded down to her waist, her expression was open and curious.

As he watched her, more and more people came out of the bush into the clearing. Most were dressed for summer, as Max chose to think of it, and all of them seemed healthy enough. None carried anything more sophisticated than a wooden spear, and none seemed to show any signs of aggression.

Max stared at them. They stared at Max. No one moved. No one spoke.

Finally Max began to get nervous, and said, in what he considered his friendliest tone of voice: "Hello!"

Six of the women instantly fled back into the bush, and one of the men fainted dead away. Max could hear excited whispering among the others. Mostly it sounded like, "He talks!"

"I bring you greetings and felicitations from the Republic," said Max when the whispering had died down.

This set off a new barrage of whispering. All Max could catch was the word "Republic", whispered with an almost religious awe.

"May I speak to your leader?" said Max after another polite pause to let them get all the whispering out of their system.

His request was greeted with riotous laughter.

"What's so funny?" he asked.

One man, a little taller and burlier than the rest, took a step forward. "*You* are our leader," he said. "It is good to know that our god has a sense of humor."

Max was about to explain that he wasn't a god, but merely an exogeologist who was pretty sure he'd discovered a rich vein of gold on this world. But then he thought about it, and decided that the inhabitants would be more willing to work longer hours at lower pay for a god than for a geologist.

"Well, you know how we gods are," said Max. "Always happy, always joking."

"You took a long time getting here," said the man. "We have sacrificed a virgin every full moon to bring you here." He paused.

"It is well that you arrived when you did," he added. "We were running out of virgins."

"Are you all the descendants of the original crew of the SOCRATES 72H?" asked Max.

"What crew?" said the man, puzzled. "We have lived on Socrates since you created the universe."

"Did you really create it in just 72 days?" asked another.

"I had some help," answered Max.

"Modesty," said the first man approvingly. "I like that in a god." There was an awkward silence. Then: "When are you taking us up to heaven with you?"

"Not right away," said Max. "All the maids and landscapers are on vacation." He could see them struggling with the concept, and added: "I thought I'd stay here with you for awhile."

"We are blessed above all other worlds!" cried the man in a spiritual frenzy. "Others doubted, but I knew if we worshipped at your shrine, sooner or later you would notice your most faithful children."

"My shrine?" asked Max.

"Certainly," he said, indicating the hull of the SOCRATES 72H. "It has been the holiest place on the planet since the day you created the universe."

"Socrates has always been my favorite world," said Max glibly. "I still remember the care I put into it, the effort I expended making every tree, flower and shrub exactly the right shape and color. I hope you are pleased with it, my children."

"It is the most perfect world in the universe!" was the reply. "We used to wonder why you populated it with so many fierce creatures that hunted and ate us, and why we are visited with a seemingly endless series of droughts, and in truth we never quite understood the reason for the periodic flooding, and of course there is the annual plague of insects that turn the sky black with their numbers, but now that you are here you can explain it to us."

"I can?" said Max, startled.

"You are a god. You can do anything."

"Oh. Right. I forgot."

"You forgot?"

"It's hard to remember when I take human form," explained Max. "You know how it is."

"So can you tell us now: why is a world made by you for your children so filled with danger?"

Max's mind raced through all the platitudes he'd read and heard over the years, trying to choose the proper one.

"That which doesn't kill you makes you stronger?" he suggested hesitantly.

"Brilliant!" said the man. "That which doesn't kill us makes us stronger!"

"It sounds good, but I don't *feel* any stronger," said the second man.

"And what about that which *does* kill us?" asked a woman.

She looked Max full in the eye. "There's a lot of it going around, as well you know."

"Gods only answer one question a day," said Max. "I'd love to tell you right now, but we have to obey the ground rules. Ask me again tomorrow."

No one challenged his statement, and Max breathed a sigh of relief.

"May we ask how long you intend to stay with us," asked another woman, "or must that question wait until tomorrow?"

"The day *after* tomorrow!" snapped the first woman. "He's answering *me* tomorrow!"

"What makes *you* more favored than me?" demanded the second woman.

"I sacrificed my virginity for him," said the first smugly.

"187 times and counting," said the second woman nastily.

"I think I can probably answer you as long as it's not an exact answer," interjected Max, trying to calm the situation and thinking one step ahead of where he was speaking. "I can tell you this much. Heaven is looking a little shopworn these days, and I thought I'd bring back some of the gold I left here to spruce it up before I showed the place off to you."

"What is gold?"

"It's a metal that I put into some underground caves, just in case I ever needed it," said Max.

"What color is it?" asked a small, bow-legged man.

"Uh... gold-colored," replied Max lamely.

"And flowers are flower-colored, but that doesn't help a man who's never seen a flower," said the man.

"I'll be there with you to show you," said Max.

"Isn't that great, men?" cried the one who seemed to be the leader. "God himself will be working side-by-side with us!"

"I had envisioned myself functioning in more of an advisory capacity," said Max uncomfortably.

"That's a god for you," said the small, bow-legged man. "Can't stand to get his hands dirty."

"Pay no attention to Ro-ger," said the leader. "I, Tho-mas, pledge my support to this heavenly project."

"And I, Don-ald, will work from dawn to dusk!" added another man.

Soon everyone but Ro-ger was pledging their allegiance to Max and his project.

"We will carry this metal up to the planet's surface for you!" cried a number of the men in unison.

"We may have to separate it from the rocks where I left it," said Max. "Fortunately, I can create the necessary tools with my godly powers." He waved his hands in the air. "*Presto Digitation!*" he intoned. "All right. All the digging equipment you need is now in my ship's cargo hold."

Within a week Max had found the richest vein of gold in the entire Albion Cluster, and a day later every able-bodied man and woman on the planet eagerly reported for work in the mines.

"Are you done yet?" asked Hector Calthrop of the Department of Alien Affairs, shifting anxiously in the chair opposite my desk.

"Not quite," I said, taking a puff of my smokeless cigar. I ordered the Servo-Mech to bring me another cup of coffee, and went back to reading:

Things went well for a few weeks. We pulled a fortune in gold out of the ground, and everyone was content just for a word or two of praise from their god. The women worked as hard as the men, and even the kids helped as best they could. It turned out that there were a lot more people on Socrates than I had thought at first. But there were no unions, no intrusive governmental bodies to deal with, no bleeding-heart do-gooders worrying about their hours and health insurance and pension benefits.

It might have gone on that way forever if I hadn't seen Doro-thi. Most of the women were pretty, but Doro-thi was so gorgeous that even I started believing in a higher power (other than myself, that is). Despite the harsh life she'd lived, her skin was soft and smooth, and she had curves in places where most girls don't even have places. She always had a smile for me (actually, everyone did; that's one of the advantages of being a god), and one day I told her not to go into the mine, but to spend the morning with me. She seemed thrilled that I had singled her out for whatever honor I had in mind, and as soon as everyone else was hard at work, I took Doro-thi off to a secluded bluff overlooking a clear lagoon. We sat down and talked for a few minutes, and then I started -- how shall I say it? -- putting the moves on her.

And she broke down and began crying. Copiously.

I figured she was just surprised to find out I had some godly needs, and I gave her a few minutes to get over it, but she began weeping and wailing even louder. Finally I asked what the problem was (I mean, hell, I'm not that ugly) and she explained that as badly as she wanted to satisfy my disgusting heavenly urges, everyone knew I could only mate with the High Priestess.

That was the first time I'd heard of any High Priestess, but in retrospect it figured. I mean, someone had to keep the notion of a god alive all these centuries, and to create some little religious rituals, and issue an occasional moral decree. So I thanked her, absolved her of any sins she'd committed since breakfast, and went off to find the High Priestess, figuring if she looked half as good as Doro-thi I could live with that.

"Half as good" was a little optimistic. She was about 400pounds on the hoof. The rags she'd been wearing for years without washing them were cleaner than she was. She was missing about half her teeth. One eye was green; the other was so bloodshot I couldn't tell what color it was. Her scruffy

hair glistened with grease, and seemed to be the most efficient insect trap on the planet.

I introduced myself, told her she'd been doing a fine job of preparing her people for my arrival, and promptly went back to the mines. But the next morning everyone knew I'd visited her, and it was explained to me, at length and ad nauseum, that the destiny of Socrates would be fulfilled only when I mated with the High Priestess and produced a godly little heir.

And that's where things stand now. They still worship me, and they still work in the mines. But they've sabotaged the ship so I can't leave. I'm sending this via the subspace radio before they figure out what the radio's for and bust the damned thing.

I get the distinct feeling that even if I take Bar-ba-ra (the High Priestess) to bed, no one's going to let me take my gold and leave. In fact, I have a horrible premonition that once an heir is on the ground, god (i.e., me) becomes expendable -- as in dead.

HELP!

Max Enright, President and Chief Deity,
Max Enright Ltd.

I put the transcription down and looked across my desk at Calthrop.

"Why did you bring this to us?" I asked.

"It's a very delicate situation," he replied. "For one thing, Beta Scaparelli III is officially uninhabited, and hence is not a member of the Republic, so we can't simply order the inhabitants to release him. Besides, we don't dare do anything to annoy them, or they could join the Federation of Worlds or one of our other rivals in the galaxy." He mopped his forehead with a shirtsleeve and continued. "And we can't just turn our backs and ignore him. It's true that he brought this situation upon himself. But there are not only large amounts of gold there, but according to his reports, there are huge deposits of heavy metals and even a considerable amount of fissionable materials."

"And?" I said.

"You're the Miracle Brigade!" he snapped. "You're supposed to be the greatest problem solvers in the Republic. Solve it!"

"Let me make sure we're perfectly clear on just what the problem is, Mr. Calthrop," I said. "You've got a bunch of people happily mining gold, and I'd be surprised if you gave a damn about Enright. So what, precisely, do you want us to do?"

"Get mining rights to the world, convince them to join the Republic, and don't let Enright screw it up!"

"Regardless of cost?" I asked.

"Just get it done."

He got up and left my office without another word.

At least he'd come to the right place. If there was ever a job made to order for the Miracle Brigade, this was it. I checked the computer to see whose name was at the top of the duty roster.

Ten minutes later I began making preparations for my trip to Socrates.

My first stop was at the agricultural world of Pollux IV, a tranquil little planet that was covered by vast farms that supplied food to a dozen nearby mining worlds. I found out that oranges were in season, bought ten thousand of them and had my purchase billed to the Republic, then waited until the fruit was loaded into my cargo hold, and took off again.

As the ship reached multiples of light speed, I sat back and reflected upon the situation. The problem with the Republic was that it never went with the flow of things; it was always confrontational. If someone said Tall, it said Short. If they said Day, it said Night. If they said No, it said Yes Or Else. Still, I couldn't complain too much; it was just that attitude that kept the Miracle Brigade in business. I always had the feeling that our erstwhile employers couldn't wait to see us fail, even though it would mean more trouble for them; it would at least prove they weren't as incompetent as we made them feel.

I didn't see it happening. The truth of the matter was that they were every bit as incompetent, and then some. They'd studied the problem on Socrates, thrown their hands up in the air, and turned it over to us -- which was just as well. Left to their own devices, they'd probably have precipitated a war and then had to explain to the public why a navy of two billion ships had fired on a planet where the most sophisticated weapon was a spear. I figured with a little luck, I could apply our methods, which had a lot more to do with common sense and accommodation than confrontation, and have it solved in less than a day.

I knew from Enright's report that there was no sense announcing my presence or asking for landing coordinates, so I had my sensor locate Enright's ship and the wreck of the SOCRATES 72H and touch down next to them. I didn't see any sense putting a lethal charge on the hull. If they wanted to sabotage the ship, the Republic would buy me a new one. But I made sure no one could damage the subspace radio.

I waited an hour before leaving the ship, because I wanted to give everyone time to pass the word and gather around it. Then, when I felt there was a sufficient crowd, I emerged from the hatch and stood on the landing platform. "Greetings and felicitations!" I said. "Is my brother here?"

"Your brother?" asked one of the men.

I nodded. "Max Enright, the god of gold mines."

"Of gold mines?" said another. "We thought he was the god of everything!"

I laughed. "That Max!" I said. "What a kidder!"

"Who are *you*?" demanded one of the women.

"I'm the god of ripe oranges," I replied.

"What are oranges?"

"Behold!" I said, pressing a control button on my belt. The hatch opened and ten thousand oranges rolled gently onto the ground.

"What do we do with them?"

"Eat them," I said. "They're my gift to you for treating my brother so well." I saw a man suddenly approaching. Since he was the only one wearing more than a loincloth, I knew it had to be Enright.

"Hello, Brother!" I called out. "I have been looking all over for you!"

He just stared at me without saying a word.

"Why have you been searching all over?" said a tall man suspiciously. "You are a god. Could you not see him all the way across the galaxy?"

"I'm just the god of oranges," I said. "You want the goddess of vision."

"We thought there was just one god," said the man.

"There was just one in the beginning," I said. "He's the father of us all."

"How many of you are there?"

I shrugged. "Thousands."

"This is very discouraging," continued the man. "We thought we were entertaining the creator of the universe."

"I'm afraid not," I said. "But I hear on the grapevine that the god of happiness -- he's the father and king of us all -- is considering paying you a visit to thank you for being so kind to my brother."

"He is?" said a woman excitedly.

"How soon can we expect him?" asked another.

"It's not that simple," I said. "I mean, we're not talking about just the god of gold mines or oranges here. We're talking about the Big Guy himself. We have to make Socrates and its people presentable to him."

"What's wrong with the way we are?" demanded the tall man.

"Nothing, if you're just meeting other men," I said. "But if you want the king of the gods to come and visit, we have to prepare the way for him."

"Right, Tho-mas,"" chimed in Enright. "He doesn't go just anywhere, you know."

"Be quiet," said Tho-mas contemptuously. "You're just the god of gold mines." He turned back to me. "What must we do?"

"Why are you listening to *him*?" demanded Enright heatedly. "He's just the god of oranges."

"But my favorite sister is the goddess of interstellar travel, and I'm sure you don't want her getting mad at you for being mean to me," I said meaningfully, and he promptly shut up. I turned back to Tho-mas. "Time has no meaning to my father. He'll come when Socrates is ready to please him, whether it takes a week or a year or a century."

"What pleases the god of happiness?" asked Tho-mas. "Besides siring thousands of offspring, that is."

"Gold makes him happy," said Max stubbornly.

"That's true," I agreed. "But so do many other things that can be found on the surface of Socrates or beneath it. My brother Max is only the god of gold mines. I think we can best prepare the way for my father by inviting the gods of heavy metals, plutonium, diamonds, and uranium and their magical machines."

"Damn it!" thundered Max. "I found this world!"

"We weren't lost," said Tho-mas.

I looked Max full in the eye. "If you'd like me to leave Socrates in your capable hands, just say the word and I'll be on my way back to Heaven."

"NO!" cried a hundred voices.

Max looked torn between disgust and defeat. Then he thought about it a little more, and it was clear defeat had won.

"I'll be happy to see all my brothers and sisters," he muttered.

"He's a very good god," I told the assembled men and women. "A bit impetuous and hot-headed, but he'll outgrow it in a few thousand years."

"So after all your mining gods arrive, will the god of happiness come next?" asked Tho-mas.

"If he's pleased with the way you have treated his children, he will send three more of his offspring -- the goddesses of education and hygiene, and the god of medicine."

"And *then* he'll come?"

"If he feels you're making sufficient progress, he will then send the god of capitalism, who will teach you how to establish an economy and join the Republic. He'll be followed by a number of heavenly emissaries who mostly wear black and carry a book called the Bible, and these emissaries will show you how to communicate with the god of happiness."

"Does he look just like you and Enright?" asked a woman.

"Well, it's true that he made man in his image," I responded. "But it's equally true that he can take any shape he pleases." I paused and looked around me. "If you're happy with all the gifts he plans to send you, he just might take the shape of Socrates itself."

"Can he do that?" asked Tho-mas dubiously.

"He can do anything," I said. "That's why he's a god."

"And what about you? What can you do?"

"Me?" I said, ordering the platform to lower me to the ground. "I'm the god of oranges." I picked up an armful and started handing them out. "Try some. They're delicious."

Pretty soon everyone was eating oranges, and Enright sidled over to me.

"Thanks for coming to my rescue," he said, "but I'm not leaving here without my gold."

"Whatever makes you happy," I said. "I suppose Socrates is as nice a place to live out your life as any."

"I don't think you understand," said Enright. "I found this place. I'm the one who discovered the gold. I have a right to it."

"Has your claim been filed and registered?" I asked.

"I haven't had a chance! They won't let me leave the planet."

I frowned. "So you're telling me that you've been extracting gold to which you have no legal claim?"

"You *know* I have!" he snapped. "That's why you're here! Someone back on Deluros VIII read my report."

"This could be serious, Enright," I said. "You've been plundering the natural resources of this world and exploiting these poor natives."

"And just what the hell are *you* doing?"

"Bringing them all the spiritual, economic, scientific and medical benefits that accrue to members of the Republic," I replied calmly.

"And what happens when the king of the gods doesn't show up?"

I shrugged. "What happened on Earth and Deluros VIII and Spica II and Greenveldt and Silverblue? Have people stopped believing in him or waiting for him to manifest himself?" I smiled. "Rumor has it he's on his way."

"That rumor's been around since the first man climbed down out of the trees," said Enright sardonically.

"There must be something to it if it's been around that long," I said. "Now I have to send a message to Deluros and tell them what to send. Will you be wanting a ride back or not?"

He glared at me for a long moment. "All right. You win," he said with a heavy sigh.

Within a month the Republic had forty mines operating at capacity. In less a year the first four schools were built, and the hospital went up a year after that.

Within a decade Socrates had voted to join the Republic, and shortly thereafter they kicked all the priests, rabbis, ministers, mullahs, and holy men off the planet. Having spoken to lesser gods, and having been told that the Big Guy was making his way there, however slowly, they saw no need for middle men. Bar-ba-ra has disdained all lesser gods and is still saving herself for him.

As for Max Enright, he realized that some things were worth more than gold, announced that he was resigning his godhood, married Doro-thi, and the last I heard was living happily ever after on Socrates.

Craphound

Cory Doctorow

Craphound had wicked yard-sale karma, for a rotten, filthy alien bastard. He was too good at panning out the single grain of gold in a raging river of uselessness for me not to like him -- respect him, anyway. But then he found the cowboy trunk. It was two months' rent to me and nothing but some squirrelly alien kitsch-fetish to Craphound.

So I did the unthinkable. I violated the Code. I got into a bidding war with a buddy. Never let them tell you that women poison friendships: in my experience, wounds from women-fights heal quickly; fights over garbage leave nothing behind but scorched earth.

Craphound spotted the sign. His karma, plus the goggles in his exoskeleton, gave him the advantage when we were doing 80 kmh on some stretch of back-highway in cottage country. He was riding shotgun while I drove, and we had the radio on to the CBC's summer-Saturday programming: eight weekends with eight hours of old radio dramas: "The Shadow," "Quiet Please," "Tom Mix," "The Crypt-Keeper" with Bela Lugosi. It was hour three, and Bogey was phoning in his performance on a radio adaptation of *The African Queen*. I had the windows of the old truck rolled down so that I could smoke without fouling Craphound's breather. My arm was hanging out the window, the radio was booming, and Craphound said "Turn around! Turn around, now, Jerry, now, turn around!"

When Craphound gets that excited, it's a sign that he's spotted a rich vein. I checked the side-mirror quickly, pounded the brakes and spun around. The transmission creaked, the wheels squealed, and then we were creeping along the way we'd come.

"There," Craphound said, gesturing with his long, skinny arm. I saw it. A wooden A-frame real-estate sign, a piece of hand-lettered cardboard stuck over top of the realtor's name:

EAST MUSKOKA VOLUNTEER FIRE-DEPT
LADIES AUXILIARY RUMMAGE SALE
SAT 25 JUNE

"Hoo-eee!" I hollered, and spun the truck onto the dirt road. I gunned the engine as we cruised along the tree-lined road, trusting Craphound to spot any deer, signs, or hikers in time to avert disaster. The sky was a perfect blue and the smells of summer were all around us. I snapped off the radio and listened to the wind rushing through the truck. Ontario is *beautiful* in the summer.

"There!" Craphound shouted. I hit the turn-off and down-shifted and then we were back on a paved road. Soon, we were rolling into a country fire-station, an ugly brick barn. The hall was lined with long, folding tables, stacked high. The mother lode!

Craphound beat me out the door, as usual. His exoskeleton is programmable, so he can record little scripts for it like: move left arm to door handle, pop it, swing legs out to running-board, jump to ground, close door, move forward. Meanwhile, I'm still making sure I've switched off the headlights and that I've got my wallet.

Two blue-haired ladies had a card-table set up out front of the hall, with a big tin pitcher of lemonade and three boxes of Tim Horton assorted donuts. That stopped us both, since we share the superstition that you *always* buy food from old ladies and little kids, as a sacrifice to the crap-gods. One of the old ladies poured out the lemonade while the other smiled and greeted us.

"Welcome, welcome! My, you've come a long way for us!"

"Just up from Toronto, ma'am," I said. It's an old joke, but it's also part of the ritual, and it's got to be done.

"I meant your friend, sir. This gentleman."

Craphound smiled without baring his gums and sipped his lemonade. "Of course I came, dear lady. I wouldn't miss it for the worlds!" His accent is pretty good, but when it comes to stock phrases like this, he's got so much polish you'd think he was reading the news.

The biddie *blushed* and *giggled*, and I felt faintly sick. I walked off to the tables, trying not to hurry. I chose my first spot, about halfway down, where things wouldn't be quite so picked-over. I grabbed an empty box from underneath and started putting stuff into it: four matched highball glasses with gold crossed bowling-pins and a line of black around the rim; an Expo '67 wall-hanging that wasn't even a little faded; a shoebox full of late sixties O-Pee-Chee hockey cards; a worn, wooden-handled steel cleaver that you could butcher a steer with.

I picked up my box and moved on: a deck of playing cards copyrighted '57, with the logo for the Royal Canadian Dairy, Bala Ontario printed on the backs; a fireman's cap with a brass badge so tarnished I couldn't read it; a three-story wedding-cake trophy for the 1974 Eastern Region Curling Championships. The cash-register in my mind was ringing, ringing, ringing. God bless the East Muskoka Volunteer Fire Department Ladies' Auxiliary.

I'd mined that table long enough. I moved to the other end of the hall. Time was, I'd start at the beginning and turn over each item, build one pile of maybes and another pile of definites, try to strategize. In time, I came to rely on instinct and on the fates, to whom I make my obeisances at every opportunity.

Let's hear it for the fates: a genuine collapsible top-hat; a white-tipped evening cane; a hand-carved cherry-wood walking stick; a beautiful black lace parasol; a wrought-iron lightning rod with a rooster on top; all of it in an elephant-leg umbrella-stand. I filled the box, folded it over, and started on another.

I collided with Craphound. He grinned his natural grin, the one that showed row on row of wet, slimy gums, tipped with writhing, poisonous suckers. "Gold! Gold!" he said, and moved along. I turned my head after him, just as he bent over the cowboy trunk.

I sucked air between my teeth. It was magnificent: a leather-bound miniature steamer trunk, the leather worked with lariats, Stetson hats, war-bonnets and six-guns. I moved toward him, and he popped the latch. I caught my breath.

On top, there was a kid's cowboy costume: miniature leather chaps, a tiny Stetson, a pair of scuffed white-leather cowboy boots with long, worn spurs affixed to the heels. Craphound moved it reverently to the table and continued to pull more magic from the trunk's depths: a stack of cardboard-bound *Hopalong Cassidy* 78s; a pair of tin six-guns with gunbelt and holsters; a silver star that said Sheriff; a bundle of *Roy Rogers* comics tied with twine, in mint condition; and a leather satchel filled with plastic cowboys and Indians, enough to re-enact the Alamo.

"Oh, my God," I breathed, as he spread the loot out on the table.

"What are these, Jerry?" Craphound asked, holding up the 78s.

"Old records, like LPs, but you need a special record player to listen to them." I took one out of its sleeve. It gleamed, scratch-free, in the overhead fluorescents.

"I got a 78 player here," said a member of the East Muskoka Volunteer Fire Department Ladies' Auxiliary. She was short enough to look Craphound in the eye, a hair under five feet, and had a skinny, rawboned look to her. "That's my Billy's things, Billy the Kid we called him. He was dotty for cowboys when he was a boy. Couldn't get him to take off that fool outfit. Nearly got him thrown out of school. He's a lawyer now, in Toronto, got a fancy office on Bay Street. I called him to ask if he minded my putting his cowboy things in the sale, and you know what? He didn't know what I was talking about! Doesn't that beat everything? He was dotty for cowboys when he was a boy."

It's another of my rituals to smile and nod and be as polite as possible to the erstwhile owners of crap that I'm trying to buy, so I smiled and nodded and examined the 78 player she had produced. In lariat script, on the top, it said, "Official Bob Wills Little Record Player," and had a crude watercolor of Bob Wills and His Texas Playboys grinning on the front. It was the kind of record player that folded up like a suitcase when you weren't using it. I'd had one as a kid, with Yogi Bear silkscreened on the front.

Billy's mom plugged the yellowed cord into a wall jack and took the 78 from me, touched the stylus to the record. A tinny ukelele played, accompanied by horse-clops, and then a narrator with a deep, whisky voice said, "Howdy, Pardners! I was just settin' down by the ole campfire. Why don't you stay an' have some beans, an' I'll tell y'all the story of how Hopalong Cassidy beat the Duke Gang when they come to rob the Santa Fe."

In my head, I was already breaking down the cowboy trunk and its contents, thinking about the minimum bid I'd place on each item at Sotheby's. Sold individually, I figured I could get over two grand for the contents. Then I thought about putting ads in some of the Japanese collectors' magazines, just for a lark, before I sent the lot to the auction house. You never can tell. A buddy I knew had sold a complete packaged set of *Welcome Back, Kotter* action figures for nearly eight grand that way. Maybe I could buy a new truck. . .

"This is wonderful," Craphound said, interrupting my reverie. "How much would you like for the collection?"

I felt a knife in my guts. Craphound had found the cowboy trunk, so that meant it was his. But he usually let me take the stuff with street-value. He was interested in *everything*, so it hardly mattered if I picked up a few scraps with which to eke out a living.

Billy's mom looked over the stuff. "I was hoping to get twenty dollars for the lot, but if that's too much, I'm willing to come down."

"I'll give you thirty," my mouth said, without intervention from my brain.

They both turned and stared at me. Craphound was unreadable behind his goggles.

Billy's mom broke the silence. "Oh, my! Thirty dollars for this old mess?"

"I will pay fifty," Craphound said.

"Seventy-five," I said.

"Oh, my," Billy's mom said.

"Five hundred," Craphound said.

I opened my mouth, and shut it. Craphound had built his stake on Earth by selling a complicated biochemical process for non-chlorophyll photosynthesis to a Saudi banker. I wouldn't ever beat him in a bidding war.

"A thousand dollars," my mouth said.

"Ten thousand," Craphound said, and extruded a roll of hundreds from somewhere in his exoskeleton.

"My Lord!" Billy's mom said. "Ten thousand dollars!"

The other pickers, the firemen, the blue haired ladies all looked up at that and stared at us, their mouths open.

"It is for a good cause." Craphound said.

"Ten thousand dollars!" Billy's mom said again.

Craphound's digits ruffled through the roll as fast as a croupier's counter, separated off a large chunk of the brown bills, and handed them to Billy's mom.

One of the firemen, a middle-aged paunchy man with a comb-over appeared at Billy's mom's shoulder.

"What's going on, Eva?" he said.

"This. . .gentleman is going to pay ten thousand dollars for Billy's old cowboy things, Tom."

The fireman took the money from Billy's mom and stared at it. He held up the top note under the light and turned it this way and that, watching the holographic stamp change from green to gold, then green again. He looked at the serial number, then the serial number of the next bill. He licked his forefinger and started counting off the bills in piles of ten. Once he had ten piles, he counted them again. "That's ten thousand dollars, all right. Thank you very much, mister. Can I give you a hand getting this to your car?"

Craphound, meanwhile, had re-packed the trunk and balanced the 78 player on top of it. He looked at me, then at the fireman.

"I wonder if I could impose on you to take me to the nearest bus station. I think I'm going to be making my own way home."

The fireman and Billy's mom both stared at me. My cheeks flushed. "Aw, c'mon," I said. "I'll drive you home."

"I think I prefer the bus," Craphound said.

"It's no trouble at all to give you a lift, friend," the fireman said.

I called it quits for the day, and drove home alone with the truck only half-filled. I pulled it into the coach-house and threw a tarp over the load and went inside and cracked a beer and sat on the sofa, watching a nature show on a desert reclamation project in Arizona, where the state legislature had traded a derelict mega-mall and a custom-built habitat to an alien for a local-area weather control machine.

The following Thursday, I went to the little crap-auction house on King Street. I'd put my finds from the weekend in the sale: lower minimum bid, and they took a smaller commission than Sotheby's. Fine for moving the small stuff.

Craphound was there, of course. I knew he'd be. It was where we met, when he bid on a case of Lincoln Logs I'd found at a fire-sale.

I'd known him for a kindred spirit when he bought them, and we'd talked afterwards, at his place, a sprawling, two-story warehouse amid a cluster of auto-wrecking yards where the junkyard dogs barked, barked, barked.

Inside was paradise. His taste ran to shrines -- a collection of fifties bar kitsch that was a shrine to liquor; a circular waterbed on a raised podium that was nearly buried under seventies bachelor pad-inalia; a kitchen that was nearly unusable, so packed it was with old barn-board furniture and rural memorabilia; a leather-appointed library straight out of a Victorian gentlemen's club; a solarium dressed in wicker and bamboo and tiki-idols. It was a hell of a place.

Craphound had known all about the Goodwills and the Sally Anns, and the auction houses, and the kitsch boutiques on Queen Street, but he still hadn't figured out where it all came from.

"Yard sales, rummage sales, garage sales," I said, reclining in a vibrating naugahyde easy-chair, drinking a glass of his pricey single-malt that he'd bought for the beautiful bottle it came in.

"But where are these? Who is allowed to make them?" Craphound hunched opposite me, his exoskeleton locked into a coiled, semi-seated position.

"Who? Well, anyone. You just one day decide that you need to clean out the basement, you put an ad in the *Star*, tape up a few signs, and voila, yard sale. Sometimes, a school or a church will get donations of old junk and sell it all at one time, as a fundraiser."

"And how do you locate these?" he asked, bobbing up and down slightly with excitement.

"Well, there're amateurs who just read the ads in the weekend papers, or just pick a neighbourhood and wander around, but that's no way to go about it. What I do is, I get in a truck, and I sniff the air, catch the scent of crap and *vroom!* I'm off like a bloodhound on a trail. You learn things over time: like stay away from Yuppie yard sales, they never have anything worth buying, just the same crap you can buy in any mall."

"Do you think I might accompany you some day?"

"Hell, sure. Next Saturday? We'll head over to Cabbagetown. Those old coach houses, you'd be amazed what people get rid of. It's practically criminal."

"I would like to go with you on next Saturday very much Mr Jerry Abington." He used to talk like that, without commas or question marks. Later, he got better, but then, it was all one big sentence.

"Call me Jerry. It's a date, then. Tell you what, though: there's a Code you got to learn before we go out. The Craphound's Code."

"What is a craphound?"

"You're lookin' at one. You're one, too, unless I miss my guess. You'll get to know some of the local craphounds, you hang around with me long enough. They're the competition, but they're also your buddies, and there're certain rules we have."

And then I explained to him all about how you never bid against a craphound at a yard-sale, how you get to know the other fellows' tastes, and when you see something they might like, you haul it out for them, and they'll do the same for you, and how you never buy something that another craphound might be looking for, if all you're buying it for is to sell it back to him. Just good form and common sense, really, but you'd be surprised how many amateurs just fail to make the jump to pro because they can't grasp it.

There was a bunch of other stuff at the auction, other craphounds' weekend treasures. This was high season, when the sun comes out and people start to clean out the cottage, the basement, the garage. There were some collectors in the crowd, and a whole whack of antique and junk dealers, and a few pickers, and me, and Craphound. I watched the bidding listlessly, waiting for my things to come up and sneaking out for smokes between lots. Craphound never once looked at me or acknowledged my presence, and I became perversely obsessed with catching his eye, so I coughed and shifted and walked past him several times, until the auctioneer glared at me, and one of the attendants asked if I needed a throat lozenge.

My lot came up. The bowling glasses went for five bucks to one of the Queen Street junk dealers; the elephant-foot fetched $350 after a spirited bidding war between an antique dealer and a collector. The collector won; the dealer took the top-hat for $100. The rest of it came up and sold, or didn't, and at end of the lot, I'd made over $800, which was rent for the month plus beer for the weekend plus gas for the truck.

Craphound bid on and bought more cowboy things -- a box of super-eight cowboy movies, the boxes moldy, the stock itself running to slime; a Navajo blanket; a plastic donkey that dispensed cigarettes out of its ass; a big neon armadillo sign.

One of the other nice things about that place over Sotheby's, there was none of this waiting thirty days to get a cheque. I queued up with the other pickers after the bidding was through, collected a wad of bills, and headed for my truck.

I spotted Craphound loading his haul into a minivan with handicapped plates. It looked like some kind of fungus was growing over the hood and side-panels. On closer inspection, I saw that the body had been covered in closely glued Lego.

Craphound popped the hatchback and threw his gear in, then opened the driver's side door, and I saw that his van had been fitted out for a legless driver, with brake and accelerator levers. A paraplegic I knew drove one just like it. Craphound's exoskeleton levered him into the seat, and I watched the eerily precise way it executed the macro that started the car, pulled the shoulder-belt, put it into drive and switched on the stereo. I heard tape-hiss, then, loud as a b-boy cruising Yonge Street, an old-timey cowboy voice: "Howdy pardners! Saddle up, we're ridin'!" Then the van backed up and sped out of the lot.

I got into the truck and drove home. Truth be told, I missed the little bastard.

Some people said that we should have run Craphound and his kin off the planet, out of the Solar System. They said that it wasn't fair for the aliens to keep us in the dark about their technologies. They say that we should have captured a ship and reverse-engineered it, built our own and kicked ass.

Some people!

First of all, nobody with human DNA could survive a trip in one of those ships. They're part of Craphound's people's bodies, as I understand it, and we just don't have the right parts. Second of all, they *were* sharing their tech with us. They just weren't giving it away. Fair trades every time.

It's not as if space was off-limits to us. We can any one of us visit their homeworld, just as soon as we figure out how. Only they wouldn't hold our hands along the way.

I spent the week haunting the "Secret Boutique," AKA the Goodwill As-Is Centre on Jarvis. It's all there is to do between yard sales, and sometimes it makes for good finds. Part of my theory of yard-sale karma holds that if I miss one day at the thrift shops, that'll be the day they put out the big score. So I hit the stores diligently and came up with crapola. I had offended the fates, I knew, and wouldn't make another score until I placated them. It was lonely work, still and all, and I missed Craphound's good eye and obsessive delight.

I was at the cash-register with a few items at the Goodwill when a guy in a suit behind me tapped me on the shoulder.

"Sorry to bother you," he said. His suit looked expensive, as did his manicure and his haircut and his wire-rimmed glasses. "I was just wondering where you found that." He gestured at a rhinestone-studded ukelele, with a cowboy hat wood-burned into the body. I had picked it up with a guilty little thrill, thinking that Craphound might buy it at the next auction.

"Second floor, in the toy section."

"There wasn't anything else like it, was there?"

"'Fraid not," I said, and the cashier picked it up and started wrapping it in newspaper.

"Ah," he said, and he looked like a little kid who'd just been told that he couldn't have a puppy. "I don't suppose you'd want to sell it, would you?"

I held up a hand and waited while the cashier bagged it with the rest of my stuff, a few old clothbound novels I thought I could sell at a used book-store, and a *Grease* belt-buckle with Olivia Newton-John on it. I led him out the door by the elbow of his expensive suit.

"How much?" I had paid a dollar.

"Ten bucks?"

I nearly said, "Sold!" but I caught myself. "Twenty."

"Twenty dollars?"

"That's what they'd charge at a boutique on Queen Street."

He took out a slim leather wallet and produced a twenty. I handed him the uke. His face lit up like a lightbulb.

It's not that my adulthood is particularly unhappy. Likewise, it's not that my childhood was particularly happy.

There are memories I have, though, that are like a cool drink of water. My grandfather's place near Milton, an old Victorian farmhouse, where the cat drank out of a milk-glass bowl; and where we sat around a rough pine table as big as my whole apartment; and where my playroom was the draughty barn with hay-filled lofts bulging with farm junk and Tarzan-ropes.

There was Grampa's friend Fyodor, and we spent every evening at his wrecking-yard, he and Grampa talking and smoking while I scampered in the twilight, scaling mountains of auto-junk. The glove-boxes yielded treasures: crumpled photos of college boys mugging in front of signs, roadmaps of far-away places. I found a guidebook from the 1964 New York World's Fair once, and a lipstick like a chrome bullet, and a pair of white leather ladies' gloves.

Fyodor dealt in scrap, too, and once, he had half of a carny carousel, a few horses and part of the canopy, paint flaking and sharp torn edges protruding; next to it, a Korean-war tank minus its turret and treads, and inside the tank were peeling old pinup girls and a rotation schedule and a crude Kilroy. The control-room in the middle of the carousel had a stack of paperback sci-fi novels, Ace Doubles that had two books bound back-to-back, and when you finished the first, you turned it over and read the other. Fyodor let me keep them, and there was a pawn-ticket in one from Macon, Georgia, for a transistor radio.

My parents started leaving me alone when I was fourteen and I couldn't keep from sneaking into their room and snooping. Mom's jewelry box had books of matches from their honeymoon in Acapulco, printed with bad palm-trees. My Dad kept an old photo in his sock drawer, of himself on muscle-beach, shirtless, flexing his biceps.

My grandmother saved every scrap of my mother's life in her basement, in dusty Army trunks. I entertained myself by pulling it out and taking it in: her Mouse Ears from the big family train-trip to Disneyland in '57, and her records, and the glittery pasteboard sign from her sweet sixteen. There were well-chewed stuffed animals, and school exercise books in which she'd practiced variations on her signature for page after page.

It all told a story. The penciled Kilroy in the tank made me see one of those Canadian soldiers in Korea, unshaven and crew-cut like an extra on M*A*S*H, sitting for bored hour after hour, staring at the pinup girls, fiddling with a crossword, finally laying it down and sketching his Kilroy quickly, before anyone saw.

The photo of my Dad posing sent me whirling through time to Toronto's Muscle Beach in the east end, and hearing the tinny AM radios playing weird psychedelic rock while teenagers lounged on their Mustangs and the girls sunbathed in bikinis that made their tits into torpedoes.

It all made poems. The old pulp novels and the pawn ticket, when I spread them out in front of the TV, and arranged them just so, they made up a poem that took my breath away.

After the cowboy trunk episode, I didn't run into Craphound again until the annual Rotary Club charity rummage sale at the Upper Canada Brewing Company. He was wearing the cowboy hat, sixguns and the silver star from the cowboy trunk. It should have looked ridiculous, but the net effect was naive and somehow charming, like he was a little boy whose hair you wanted to muss.

I found a box of nice old melamine dishes, in various shades of green – four square plates, bowls, salad-plates, and a serving tray. I threw them in the duffel-bag I'd brought and kept browsing, ignoring Craphound as he charmed a salty old Rotarian while fondling a box of leather-bound books.

I browsed a stack of old Ministry of Labour licenses -- barber, chiropodist, bartender, watchmaker. They all had pretty seals and were framed in stark green institutional metal. They all had different names, but all from one family, and I made up a little story to entertain myself, about the proud mother saving her sons' accreditations and framing hanging them in the spare room with their diplomas. "Oh, George Junior's just opened his own barbershop, and little Jimmy's still fixing watches. . ."

I bought them.

In a box of crappy plastic My Little Ponies and Barbies and Care Bears, I found a leather Indian headdress, a wooden bow-and-arrow set, and a fringed buckskin vest. Craphound was still buttering up the leather books' owner. I bought them quick, for five bucks.

"Those are beautiful," a voice said at my elbow. I turned around and smiled at the snappy dresser who'd bought the uke at the Secret Boutique. He'd gone casual for the weekend, in an expensive, L.L. Bean button-down way.

"Aren't they, though."

"You sell them on Queen Street? Your finds, I mean?"

"Sometimes. Sometimes at auction. How's the uke?"

"Oh, I got it all tuned up," he said, and smiled the same smile he'd given me when he'd taken hold of it at Goodwill. "I can play 'Don't Fence Me In' on it." He looked at his feet. "Silly, huh?"

"Not at all. You're into cowboy things, huh?" As I said it, I was overcome with the knowledge that this was "Billy the Kid," the original owner of the cowboy trunk. I don't know why I felt that way, but I did, with utter certainty.

"Just trying to re-live a piece of my childhood, I guess. I'm Scott," he said, extending his hand.

Scott? I thought wildly. *Maybe it's his middle name?* "I'm Jerry."

The Upper Canada Brewery sale has many things going for it, including a beer garden where you can sample their wares and get a good BBQ burger. We gently gravitated to it, looking over the tables as we went.

"You're a pro, right?" he asked after we had plastic cups of beer.

"You could say that."

"I'm an amateur. A rank amateur. Any words of wisdom?"

I laughed and drank some beer, lit a cigarette. "There's no secret to it, I think. Just diligence: you've got to go out every chance you get, or you'll miss the big score."

He chuckled. "I hear that. Sometimes, I'll be sitting in my office, and I'll just *know* that they're putting out a piece of pure gold at the Goodwill and that someone else will get to it before my lunch. I get so wound up, I'm no good until I go down there and hunt for it. I guess I'm hooked, eh?"

"Cheaper than some other kinds of addictions."

"I guess so. About that Indian stuff -- what do you figure you'd get for it at a Queen Street boutique?"

I looked him in the eye. He may have been something high-powered and cool and collected in his natural environment, but just then, he was as eager and nervous as a kitchen-table poker-player at a high-stakes game.

"Maybe fifty bucks," I said.

"Fifty, huh?" he asked.

"About that," I said.

"Once it sold," he said.

"There is that," I said.

"Might take a month, might take a year," he said.

"Might take a day," I said.

"It might, it might." He finished his beer. "I don't suppose you'd take forty?"

I'd paid five for it, not ten minutes before. It looked like it would fit Craphound, who, after all, was wearing Scott/Billy's own boyhood treasures as we spoke. You don't make a living by feeling guilty over eight hundred percent markups. Still, I'd angered the fates, and needed to redeem myself.

"Make it five," I said.

He started to say something, then closed his mouth and gave me a look of thanks.

He took a five out of his wallet and handed it to me. I pulled the vest and bow and headdress out my duffel.

He walked back to a shiny black Jeep with gold detail work, parked next to Craphound's van. Craphound was building onto the Lego body, and the hood had a miniature Lego town attached to it.

Craphound looked around as he passed, and leaned forward with undisguised interest at the booty. I grimaced and finished my beer.

I met Scott/Billy three times more at the Secret Boutique that week.

He was a lawyer, who specialized in alien-technology patents. He had a practice on Bay Street, with two partners, and despite his youth, he was the senior man.

I didn't let on that I knew about Billy the Kid and his mother in the East Muskoka Volunteer Fire Department Ladies' Auxiliary. But I felt a bond with him, as though we shared an unspoken secret. I pulled any cowboy finds for him, and he developed a pretty good eye for what I was after and returned the favor.

The fates were with me again, and no two ways about it. I took home a ratty old Oriental rug that on closer inspection was a 19th century hand-knotted Persian; an upholstered Turkish footstool; a collection of hand-painted silk Hawaiiana pillows and a carved Meerschaum pipe. Scott/Billy found the last for me, and it cost me two dollars. I knew a collector who would pay thirty in an eye-blink, and from then on, as far as I was concerned, Scott/Billy was a fellow craphound.

"You going to the auction tomorrow night?" I asked him at the checkout line.

"Wouldn't miss it," he said. He'd barely been able to contain his excitement when I told him about the Thursday night auctions and the bargains to be had there. He sure had the bug.

"Want to get together for dinner beforehand? The Rotterdam's got a good patio."

He did, and we did, and I had a glass of framboise that packed a hell of a kick and tasted like fizzy raspberry lemonade; and doorstopper fries and a club sandwich.

I had my nose in my glass when he kicked my ankle under the table. "Look at that!"

It was Craphound in his van, cruising for a parking spot. The Lego village had been joined by a whole postmodern spaceport on the roof, with a red-and-blue castle, a football-sized flying saucer, and a clown's head with blinking eyes.

I went back to my drink and tried to get my appetite back.

"Was that an extee driving?"

"Yeah. Used to be a friend of mine."

"He's a picker?"

"Uh-huh." I turned back to my fries and tried to kill the subject.

"Do you know how he made his stake?"

"The chlorophyll thing, in Saudi Arabia."

"Sweet!" he said. "Very sweet. I've got a client who's got some secondary patents from that one. What's he go after?"

"Oh, pretty much everything," I said, resigning myself to discussing the topic after all. "But lately, the same as you, cowboys and Injuns."

He laughed and smacked his knee. "Well, what do you know? What could he possibly want with the stuff?"

"What do they want with any of it? He got started one day when we were cruising the Muskokas," I said carefully, watching his face. "Found a trunk of old cowboy things at a rummage sale. East Muskoka Volunteer Fire Department Ladies' Auxiliary." I waited for him to shout or startle. He didn't.

"Yeah? A good find, I guess. Wish I'd made it."

I didn't know what to say to that, so I took a bite of my sandwich.

Scott continued. "I think about what they get out of it a lot. There's nothing we have here that they couldn't make for themselves. I mean, if they picked up and left today, we'd still be making sense of everything they gave us in a hundred years. You know, I just closed a deal for a biochemical computer that's no-shit 10,000 times faster than anything we've built out of silicon. You know what the extee took in trade? Title to a defunct fairground outside of Calgary-- they shut it down ten years ago because the midway was too unsafe to ride. Doesn't that beat all? This thing is worth a billion dollars right out of the gate, I mean, within twenty-four hours of the deal closing, the seller can turn it into the GDP of Bolivia. For a crummy real-estate dog that you couldn't get five grand for!"

It always shocked me when Billy/Scott talked about his job. It was easy to forget that he was a high-powered lawyer when we were jawing and fooling around like old craphounds. I wondered if maybe he *wasn't* Billy the Kid; I couldn't think of any reason for him to be playing it all so close to his chest.

"What the hell is some extee going to do with a fairground?"

Craphound got a free Coke from Lisa at the check-in when he made his appearance. He bid high, but shrewdly, and never pulled ten-thousand-dollar stunts. The bidders were wandering the floor, previewing that week's stock, and making notes to themselves.

I rooted through a box-lot full of old tins, and found one with a buckaroo at the Calgary Stampede, riding a bucking bronc. I picked it up and stood to inspect it. Craphound was behind me.

"Nice piece, huh?" I said to him.

"I like it very much," Craphound said, and I felt my cheeks flush.

"You're going to have some competition tonight, I think," I said, and nodded at Scott/Billy. "I think he's Billy; the one whose mother sold us -- you – the cowboy trunk."

"Really?" Craphound said, and it felt like we were partners again, scoping out the competition. Suddenly I felt a knife of shame, like I was betraying Scott/Billy somehow. I took a step back.

"Jerry, I am very sorry that we argued."

I sighed out a breath I hadn't known I was holding in. "Me, too."

"They're starting the bidding. May I sit with you?"

And so the three of us sat together, and Craphound shook Scott/Billy's hand and the auctioneer started into his harangue.

It was a night for unusual occurrences. I bid on a piece, something I told myself I'd never do. It was a set of four matched Li'l Orphan Annie Ovaltine glasses, like Grandma's had been, and seeing them in the auctioneer's hand took me right back to her kitchen, and endless afternoons passed with my coloring books and weird old-lady hard candies and Liberace albums playing in the living room.

"Ten," I said, opening the bidding.

"I got ten, ten,ten, I got ten, who'll say twenty, who'll say twenty, twenty for the four."

Craphound waved his bidding card, and I jumped as if I'd been stung.

"I got twenty from the space cowboy, I got twenty, sir will you say thirty?"

I waved my card.

"That's thirty to you sir."

"Forty," Craphound said.

"Fifty," I said even before the auctioneer could point back to me. An old pro, he settled back and let us do the work.

"One hundred," Craphound said.

"One fifty," I said.

The room was perfectly silent. I thought about my overextended MasterCard, and wondered if Scott/Billy would give me a loan.

"Two hundred," Craphound said.

Fine, I thought. Pay two hundred for those. I can get a set on Queen Street for thirty bucks.

The auctioneer turned to me. "The bidding stands at two. Will you say two-ten, sir?"

I shook my head. The auctioneer paused a long moment, letting me sweat over the decision to bow out.

"I have two. Do I have any other bids from the floor? Any other bids? Sold, $200, to number 57." An attendant brought Craphound the glasses. He took them and tucked them under his seat.

I was fuming when we left. Craphound was at my elbow. I wanted to punch him. I'd never punched anyone in my life, but I wanted to punch him.

We entered the cool night air and I sucked in several lungfuls before lighting a cigarette.

"Jerry," Craphound said.

I stopped, but didn't look at him. I watched the taxis pull in and out of the garage next door instead.

"Jerry, my friend," Craphound said.

"What?" I said, loud enough to startle myself. Scott, beside me, jerked as well.

"We're going. I wanted to say goodbye, and to give you some things that I won't be taking with me."

"What?" I said again, Scott just a beat behind me.

"My people. We're going. It has been decided. We've gotten what we came for."

Without another word, he set off towards his van. We followed along behind, shell-shocked.

Craphound's exoskeleton executed another macro and slid the panel-door aside, revealing the cowboy trunk.

"I wanted to give you this. I will keep the glasses."

"I don't understand," I said.

"You're all leaving?" Scott asked, with a note of urgency.

"It has been decided. We'll go over the next twenty-four hours."

"But *why?"* Scott said, sounding almost petulant.

"It's not something that I can easily explain. As you must know, the things we gave you were trinkets to us. Almost worthless. We traded them for something that was almost worthless to you -- a fair trade, you'll agree -- but it's time to move on."

Craphound handed me the cowboy trunk. Holding it, I smelled the lubricant from his exoskeleton and the smell of the attic it had been mummified in before making its way into his hands. I felt like I almost understood.

"This is for me," I said slowly, and Craphound nodded encouragingly. "This is for me, and you're keeping the glasses. And I'll look at this and feel. . ."

"You understand," Craphound said, looking somehow relieved.

And I *did.* I understood that an alien wearing a cowboy hat and sixguns and giving them away was a poem and a story, and a thirtyish bachelor trying to spend half a month's rent on four glasses so that he could remember his Grandma's kitchen was a story and a poem, and that the disused fairground outside Calgary was a story and a poem, too.

"You're craphounds!" I said. "All of you!"

Craphound smiled so I could see his gums and I put down the cowboy trunk and clapped my hands.

Scott recovered from his shock by spending the night at his office, crunching numbers, talking on the phone, and generally getting while the getting was good. He had an edge. No one else knew that they were going.

He went pro later that week, opened a chi-chi boutique on Queen Street, and hired me on as chief picker and factum factotum.

Scott was not Billy the Kid. Just another Bay Street shyster with a cowboy jones. From the way they come down and spend, there must be a million of them.

Our draw in the window is a beautiful mannequin I found, straight out of the Fifties, a little boy we call The Beaver. He dresses in chaps and a sheriff's badge and sixguns and a miniature Stetson and cowboy boots with worn spurs, and rests one foot on a beautiful miniature steamer trunk whose leather is worked with cowboy motifs.

He's not for sale at any price.

Human Sacrifice for Fun and Profit

Ernest Hogan

They were not dressed in black when they came for Victor Theremin.

"It's unlocked. Come in. I've been expecting you," Theremin said, before they could knock on the door of the geodesic dome that was studded with solar panels and satellite dishes.

Their suits were a nondescript grey. Mirrorshades hid their eyes. Wireless devices stuck out of their ears. One of them was not a man.

They entered, hands hovering around their guns.

Theremin wore a tattered guayabera shirt, swim trunks, and flip-flops, and was watching a video of a bullfight on his computer.

"What?" he said. "A lung kill? Why'd they bother to post this? Some people just have no sense of aesthetics!"

"Victor Theremin?" asked the male.

"Of course! You know damn well who I am!"

"You have to come with us." said the female.

"Back in the old days," Theremin said, "we used to say that just because you were paranoid didn't mean that they weren't out to get you. Now I realize that just because they come to get you doesn't necessarily mean you're paranoid."

He shook his Einstein hair and gave a smile that tweaked his Villa moustache.

"Just come with us, sir," said the male.

The female leaned forward and looked grim.

"Who are you?" Theremin asked as her hand crushed his shoulder.

"You mean you haven't figured that out yet?" The male stared through his mirrorshades.

"I have some theories." Theremin reached to shut down his computer.

Suddenly, there was a gun in his ear.

"Just leave it running." said the female.

Theremin got up. "So, no handcuffs?"

"We are not law enforcement," said the male.

"I figured that. Nothing as mundane as some kind of government coming for my ass. And you probably aren't the advance guard of some interplanetary invasion either."

The female lead him out the door. "So, you really are a science fiction writer."

"And damn proud of it, too." Theremin looked skyward and waved.

The male drew his gun. "What are you doing?"

"Oh, I always wave at the spy satellites when I go outside. They can see me, but they can't figure out what's going on in my head."

"Yes," said the female. "And that's the problem."

They led him to a strange car. It was silver, and didn't seem to have any place for an engine. With a tweet from a handheld device, the doors opened.

"Cool vehicle," said Theremin as the seatbelts automatically grabbed him.

"Our employers provided it," said the male.

"What does it run on?"

"We're not allowed to say," said the female.

The car started moving. There was no steering wheel. And no engine noise.

Theremin looked out the windows from the back seat and sighed. "Another beautiful morning in Valle Perdido, Baja California! It's heating up, too. Hot weather gets me in the mood for daring feats of the imagination!"

The dirt road wound through strange trees. They looked like giant, stretched-out, upside-down carrots, studded with branches that looked like antennae. Except they were green.

Theremin smiled. "Ah! Boojums! My favorite tree! Look like they belong on Mars, don't they? Every time I go down this road, I expect to see four-armed, fifteen-foot-tall green guys."

His captors did not react.

"Yeah, you two probably never read Edgar Rice Burroughs, or even William Burroughs. Two guys who really blew my mind. And that's a good thing."

"I've read a lot of sci-fi," said the male. "Edgar was corny, and William was incomprehensible."

"You probably don't like to have your mind blown."

"That's right. I prefer it when things make sense."

"You must be unhappy most of the time."

"I've heard of most science fiction writers, Theremin. So how come I never heard of you until we were ordered to come get you?"

"I'm what you call a *cult* author. And the rumors of cannibalism and human sacrifice have been greatly exaggerated."

"So you mean that you have a small but fanatical following," said the male, "not that anybody sacrifices virgins to you."

"Well . . . " Theremin did the moustache-tweaking smile. "Only a few have been actual virgins so far . . ."

"What?" The female blurted.

"My, uh, followers are quite loyal, and supportive. They manage to fix me up with young, female companions . . ."

"Prostitutes?"

"No. I think of them as groupies. A politically correct term would be interns."

The male smiled. The female frowned.

"It's really not all that sordid. Young women who are impressed by my work are invited to come spend a few weeks with me. I get my needs satisfied. They get valuable educational experience. In a few years they'll start turning the sorry mess we've made of the world upside-down."

The female just shook her head. "It probably traumatizes them."

Theremin's expression parodied humility. "What I really do is blow their minds."

"You really like that 'mind-blowing' term, don't you?" asked the male.

"It's a way of life for me."

"So," the female asked, "just why would anybody provide you with these . . . interns?"

"My fans find my work inspiring. They do things to keep it coming."

"Keep it coming?" The male's expression got predatory. "You haven't published anything in years. And the best quote I could find on you called you the Kilgore Trout of your generation. Most of the people who've heard of you think you're dead."

"Kilgore is extremely underrated. And I haven't published in ordinary markets lately, because I've found a better way of doing things."

Both sets of mirrorshade-hidden eyes looked back at him through the rearview, giving him multiple view of his own smiling image.

"I send my stories to my fans directly through encrypted blipmail."

"How do you make a living? We find no record of employment for you since the Reagan administration."

"Fans subscribe. We communicate. Help each other out."

The male contemplated the desert. The boojums were thinning out. "People pay you directly?"

"Yeah."

"Look, I've read your work. Your novel *Chupacabra, Mon Amour* is about a Chicano mad scientist. Totally unbelievable!"

"Actually, I know a few."

"*Lobotomy Leftovers*, your online serial, doesn't make any sense."

"You're just one of those people who don't get it."

"And the short story 'Genitalien' isn't even good pornography."

"It's not porn, it's science fiction."

"I still don't see why anyone would pay you directly for the drivel you write, much less allow you to afford that dome full of electronics back there."

"Yet, the dome is there."

The male looked past the rear window at the dirt road that twisted into the rocky hills. The dome was no longer visible.

"Yeah. You got me there. The dome exists. I didn't expect it to be there. When they told me about you, I thought you were a joke."

"The joke is I'm one of the few science fiction writers who's doing the job these days."

"And just what is 'the job?'" asked the female.

"Blowing people's minds with daring feats of the imagination that keeps them on their toes when the future catches them by surprise. It's like mental kung fu."

"But," the male said, "these days we all have so much access to information ..."

"Yet nobody was ready for the twenty-first century when it came crashing down on their heads! It's all about human sacrifice for fun and profit! Incredible! Even I wouldn't have dared dreamed that journalists would be using the word 'beheaded' so often."

"And," the male went on, "sci-fi is more popular than ever."

"Oh yeah – corporate-owned alternate universes for the cubicle-dwellers to retreat into, like a bull afraid come out of its querencia."

"What?" The male and female said simultaneously.

"Nobody in the so-called civilized world pays attention to bullfighting any more. It's a place in the ring where the bull feels comfortable, it hunkers down there, refuses to fight."

"And what's wrong with that?" asked the female.

"It's boring. Science fiction should be like the pasa doble between the bull and matador, getting blood on the pretty shirt. Or when they have to bring out banderillas with firecrackers on them, to startle the creature into action."

"Disgusting," said the female.

"Hey, I never claimed I was doing anything civilized."

"So your fans find what you do more entertaining than *American Idol?*" asked the male.

Theremin just laughed.

"And who are these people," asked the female, "who can afford to support you?"

"Uh-oh,! We're getting into Super-Duper-Tip-Top-Secret-Security Clearance stuff here. I'll have to swear you both the secrecy. Both of you, hold up hold up your right hands. " He held up his own right hand, and grinned.

They glared back at him through the rearview mirror.

"Okay, I'll just have to trust you. My fans officially call themselves the Intergalactic Mad Scientist Secret Society."

"Intergalactic?" The male sounded skeptical. The female agreed silently.

"You gotta admire them for that kind of ambition."

"Mad?" The female smirked.

"Well, they're not necessarily mad, and not necessarily scientists. Like Salvador Dalí said, 'The only difference between myself and a madman is that I am *not* mad.'"

"You really expect us to believe this?" Asked the male.

"No. Me and Baron Munchausen have the same problem."

"Who?" They both asked.

Theremin laughed. "Believe it or not, it's true. Some people like my weird ideas, they get weird ideas of their own, and they go out and do weird things. That's what science fiction is really about!"

"That sounds . . . dangerous," said the female

"Sure is. Ain't it great?"

"But there is a kind of twisted logic to it." The male turned to his partner. "Maybe that's why they want him."

The smirky expression left Theremin's face. "They? Now we're talking. Who are they? Come to think of it, who are you? You got any ID?"

"We aren't law enforcement, or affiliated with any kind of government," explained the male.

"That goes for me, too," said Theremin.

"We don't need to show you any ID," said the female.

"I've always been a we-don't-need-no-stinking-badges kind of guy myself. So who are these mysterious 'they' who want me so desperately?"

They looked at each other through the mirrorshades. The gadgets in their ears made a twittering noise. Their mouths dropped open.

Theremin amused himself by humming Frank Zappa's "Let's Make the Water Turn Black."

"They have decided to let us tell you about them." The female finally said, but seemed surprised.

"Well ain't that pretty damn considerate of them! Whatever they are!"

"This a very rare thing," the male explained. "If the wrong people found out about them . . ."

"This could start sounding like a cornball science fiction story." Theremin smiled and scratched his Einstein hair. "Maybe they could just make life easier and talk to me directly."

"No no no no no!" said the female.

"She's right – you wouldn't want that," said the male. "It's extremely difficult."

"Aw, come on," Theremin said, "how hard could it be?"

The female groaned.

The male settled down in his seat and explained. "Imagine having a conversation with a group of brilliant, but autistic children. They're smarter than us, but there are gaps in their understanding. Humor is beyond them. Sensory input confuses them. They don't get any cultural references. They take everything literally. A single metaphor can result in hours of explaining . . ."

" . . . that never quite succeeds," the female said. "And they never stop talking to each other, like they're always on the cell phone."

"We have specialists who talk to them, but they burn out fast," said the male.

"Now that's weird. Are they from Outer Space?"

The male laughed. "They come from *this* planet. We created them."

"Oh. AIs! It finally happened. Could the singularity be far behind?"

They shuddered.

"Don't tell me it's already here!" This time Theremin sounded scared.

"No," said the female. "It's not."

"They haven't started designing their own replacements yet," said the male.

"Why not?" asked Theremin.

"They are . . . intimidated," explained the male.

"By what?"

"Life."

"Why?"

"They are artificial intelligences." The female sounded like she felt sorry for them. "They were designed to be logical, to make sense, to figure things out."

"So they look out into the world and they see us going merrily nuts," said the male.

"And they're disturbed?' Theremin had a twinkle in his eye.

"Damned right," said the male.

"Yes! Yes! Yes!" Theremin jumped up and down as far as the seatbelt would let him. "I'm right! My theory is right! Some people owe me money!"

"What are you jabbering about?" asked the female.

"I've been talking to people. I've said that the singularity isn't going be any kind of big, fat, hairy deal."

"But," the male said, "these AIs are smarter than us."

Theremin made a noise like a wet fart. "I've been around a lot of really smart people in my life, and one thing I can tell you. Being smarter really doesn't do you much good. After a certain point, it just makes you dysfunctional. You know how many geniuses need keepers ? Sometimes whole teams of keepers?"

"But they think faster than us!" said the female. "And they have access to more information than all previous generations of humans . . ."

"So? Even if they are better than we are at sorting through it, what are they supposed to be sorting for? Once they've gobbled up the sum total of all knowledge, what are they going to do with it? I think they'll just build themselves some interstellar hot rods and go suck supernovas."

The male groaned. "I wish you hadn't said that."

"They don't understand sexuality," said the female. "But they feel the need to understand it because it's a primary part of human motivation. They want to create some way for them to experience it, for the insight."

"Glad to be of service!" said Theremin.

The male reluctantly shook his head. "That is the problem. They could create improved versions of themselves, but they're not sure if they want to."

"I hate to say it," said the female, "but they're neurotic."

"Of course they are, like it or not, they're stuck with us as the reference point for what they're learning, and they don't relate to us. Trying to understand us probably scares the crap out of them, and they don't know how to be scared."

"I still don't see why they think studying you will help."

"Uh-humph!" Theremin beamed with pride. "I guess they just have good taste! So when do I meet them? Bring 'em on! I can hardly wait to blow their minds!"

Both the male and female got quiet.

By this time desert was extremely barren. No plants studded the rocky ground. It was as if the boojums were afraid of this area, which looked more like part of the Moon or Mars than the Earth.

"Should we tell him?" the female asked.

"I don't know, what would they think?" he replied.

"Do we ever know what they think?"

"Good point."

"So why not? Besides, he's pissing me off."

"Pissing people off is one my hobbies," said Theremin.

The car made its own merry way down the dirt path that rapidly melted away into the desert. They turned in their seats and grinned at him.

"You're not really going to talk to them." The female looked sadistic.

"Like we said, communicating with them is difficult," explained the male. "Trained specialists get burned out in no time."

"Bring 'em on! I'm all about bizarre communications!"

"Sorry," the female said. "That's not the way they want it."

Theremin fidgeted in his seat. "So just how do they want it?"

The male turned grim. "You have to realize, they aren't human. The way they interact with the universe – their very mode of existence is different. They see this as a problem, and they have devised a solution."

"A final solution?"

The female gave a little laugh. "In a way. They think that what you know about living in a crazy world seems to be the one coherent theme in your work – "

"My god!" cried Theremin. "They get it! They really are awfully smart!"

" – And this is contained in your brain. So they believe they can access this information by analyzing your brain."

"Now they're being nerdy again," said Theremin. "Confusing hardware with software."

"They aren't sure if *they're* hardware or software," said the male.

"But then, do we know which *we* are . . .? " Theremin said. "Hey! Don't tell me they want to eat my brain!"

"They see it as a nano-level deconstructive analysis process," said the female.

"The state of the art in technology," said Theremin, "and they act like headhunters."

"Yeah," said the male.

"Disturbing, isn't it?" said the female.

Theremin was speechless. A rare event.

The car pulled into a crater-like valley, then came to stop.

"You know," Theremin said, "I have another theory, I think that if human beings have a purpose in this universe, it's to go against nature and prove what's possible. If something is possible, sooner or later there'll be some human crazy and resourceful enough to actually do it! It doesn't matter if it should or shouldn't be done, it's what we do. Hell, we may destroy the world, or the universe – just to see the fireworks!"

A sun roof opened over Theremin's head.

"Are you trying to scare them?" asked the female.

"No." Theremin's seat rose up through the sun roof. "I'm trying to make this easier for the two of you."

"Don't be ridiculous," said the male. "We've been working for them for a while. We've seen some really weird stuff."

Theremin let out a little laugh. "You forget, weird stuff is my business. And one thing I've learned is to never get the idea that you've seen it all."

With a sonic boom, something zoomed down from the upper atmosphere. It dropped like a meteor, then came to an abrupt halt about fifty feet over Theremin's head. It was saucer-shaped, and glittered in the desert sun.

"Impressive," said Theremin. "And you still say they're from this planet."

"Of course," said the male. "That's a customized CIA-surplus saucer."

A hole dilated on the underside of the saucer. Out of it, an articulate metal cable moved like a tentacle, reaching for Theremin with a complicated metal claw.

"Hold still," said the female. "They're going to extract your brain. If you struggle, they'll just take your entire head."

"They are headhunters! Like I said, human sacrifice for fun and profit! Human sacrifice is about giving your all. Always give your all, after all, it's all you've got! Guess I better end this charade." Theremin reached under his shirt.

"You won't be able to get out of those seatbelts," warned the male.

"I don't have to." He pressed a finger into his navel. They heard a click, then a buzz.

Theremin's head exploded.

The male and female braced themselves to be showered with brain and skull fragments.

With trembling fingers, the female picked a chunk of smoking debris out of her hair. "Hey – this isn't the wet stuff. It's like part of a machine. He was a robot?"

"More like an android," said the male. "What Philip K. Dick called 'an artificial construct masquerading as human.'"

"I never though he was for real," said the female.

The claw seemed to sniff the smoky ruin of the android's neck. Finding nothing, it retracted into the saucer.

Suddenly, their handheld devices rang.

Flipping them open, they saw Theremin on the tiny screens.

"Greetings from the Venusian jungle!" He was surrounded by young women wearing nothing but elaborate body paint and carrying strange weapons. "Or maybe it's Valle Perdido in the Upper Amazon, or Borneo, or the Philippines, or Nepal, or even Texas. Have fun figuring it out. And remember that rumors of my death are always greatly exaggerated. Tell your employers if they think this is something, wait till they read my next novel, *Let 'Em Suck Supernovas*, I'll get back to work on it soon . . ." He looked at the women. ". . . if I don't get too distracted here. And don't think they're getting off cheap, this little bit of educational blowmind performance art is gonna cost them. I'll send someone along to collect, soon!"

The screens went blank. A high-pitched squeal bit through their earpieces. They had to remove them.

The squeal subsided into static. When they put their earpieces back in, the static formed into an approximation of a human voice that said:

"WHATEVER HE ASKS, PAY HIM DOUBLE!"

The Great VÜDÜ Linux Teen Zombie Massacree

Lucy A. Snyder

Bob and I attracted a pack of zombies when we stopped to fuel up and check our e-mail at the Gas & Grep in Buffalo Springs. I hoped we'd lost them, but hope was all I had. Bob said they were the fresh remains of a high school football team who'd been drowned and de-souled by water daemons at a lakeside party.

Young, strong corpses have the speed and stamina to run down a deer. Until the sun and wind finally turned their flesh to stinky jerky, they'd be dangerous enough to make a vampire crap bats. And fresh zombies are persistent as porn site pop-up ads. If they take a fancy to the smell of your blood, they might track you for days, stopping only if live meat falls right in their laps

It'd be months before they got the Dead Man Shamble and could be taken out with a well-placed head shot. Of course, with the right software and hardware, you could kill even the most problem zombie, but that was some fairly arcane stuff, even for experienced hackers.

If my editor was right, Bob was one of only about five genuine cyberspiritual experts in the U.S. But so far he seemed more like a second-rate grease monkey than a computer guru. I had my doubts.

"Maybe we should go back to the Gas & Grep," I suggested. "Bubba said he had a sick badger in one of his pens. Wouldn't this work better with a fresh animal?"

More important, Bubba had plenty of guns and ammunition; all I had was a small 6-shot Beretta in the thigh pocket of my cargo pants. Bob had a small deer rifle in the gun rack of his cab. Not nearly enough firepower if the zombie teen squad showed up.

"'Taint no challenge, little lady," Bob said, his voice dripping with scorn and tobacco juice. "Any fool with a copy o' Red Hat and a pair of pliers can put Linux on a live badger, or even a fresh-kilt one."

Bob hit a pothole, and I nearly lost my grip on my Treo PDA. My nice shiny new Nokia phone had fallen out of my pocket when the dead kid in the tattered Godsmack tee shirt was chasing me through the parking lot by the gas pumps, and I'd be damned if I was going to lose anything else on this trip.

I was going to kill my editor for sending me on this Texas Hellride. Absolutely kill her. Or at least demand a paid vacation. I could still hear Wendy's simpering wheedle: "The highway patrol says the Lubbock area is all clear; you'll be perfectly safe, Sarah."

Safe, my ass.

Bob was warming to his rant. "This zombie business is war. War, little lady, the kind Patton never dreamt of. We are fighting the gall-darned Forces o' Darkness. We gotta use some serious finesse, and there ain't nothing that spells finesse like installing a home defense system on a dead badger. You write that down, little lady. The readers o' MacHac need to know this stuff if they're gonna keep them an' theirs safe."

I dutifully typed it down on my Treo. I'd gotten pretty quick with the thumb keyboard, but as a precaution against being dropped in the mud I'd stuck the PDA down in a unlubricated clear polyurethane condom and tied off the open end with a rubber band. The condom, though dry, was still pretty slick, adding an extra layer of challenge to note-taking.

"Hot damn, come to papa!" Bob abruptly swerved over onto the shoulder and slammed on the brakes. The Ford slewed to a stop in the caliche beside a stand of mesquites.

In the glow of the headlights was a dead badger, all four legs stiff in the air. It was on the large side, maybe close to twenty pounds. Bob hopped out of the truck and ran over to the badger, turning it over and feeling around in the blood-matted fur.

"The legs and spine and skull are in right fine shape," he yelled back to me, as excited as a ten-year-old on Christmas morning. "I can't feel nothing but some broke ribs. This'll do!"

He tossed the badger into the bed of the truck, and soon we were speeding back to Bob's shop.

Bob's Computer Shack was wedged in between a hair salon and a Subway sandwich shop in a little roadside strip. The big storefront windows on all the shops had been boarded up with plywood sheets and reinforced with two-by-fours and rebar; all the shopkeepers were relying on neon "Open" signs to tell passersby that they were carrying on with business in the face of the zombie apocalypse.

I followed Bob into the shop and he locked and barred the door behind us. The air smelled of dust and plastic with a faint metallic stink from a burned-out monitor he'd hauled in for parts. Soon, it was all going to reek of rotten badger. Bob carried the carcass over to a work table he'd already cleared off and covered with a long sheet of butcher paper. He wiped his hands off on his overalls and pulled out an old tangerine iBook, which he set on the other end of the table. I pulled out my Treo to take notes.

"Okay, first the easy crap: puttin' the Duppy card in the iBook so's we can get OSX to talk to the badger," Bob said. "I already downloaded a copy of FleshGolem from the Apple site — it's in the Utilities section."

Bob pulled what looked like a wireless notebook card out of a drawer of the table. It had a hinged lid and a clear cover over what looked like a small, shallow ivory box inlaid in the card.

"Next, you take some hair and blood from the critter and put them in this here compartment." He popped the cover open and smeared a hairy clot into the box.

Bob lifted the keyboard off the iBook to reveal the Airport slot. He slid the Duppy card inside, replaced the keyboard set the iBook aside.

I heard a thump and a shriek from the hair salon next door.

"Marla, git yer shotgun!" I heard a woman holler.

The woman sounded a little like Wendy, though the only time I'd ever really heard my editor scream was when a college intern lost an entire set of page proofs. Mostly she just took on a fakey-sweet patronizing tone when she thought you'd screwed up:

"Well, we'll do this better next time, now won't we, Sarah?" She talked down to practically everyone like we were preschoolers. No wonder she'd been divorced twice.

Damn her for sending me out here. If I survived this, I was gonna demand vacation *and* a shiny new workstation

"Okay, now we gotta install the Duppy security antenna," Bob said, apparently oblivious to the shouting next door. "You can run your badger without it, but it'd be pretty easy for someone to hack him if they could get some blood and hair offa it."

I jumped as the shotgun boomed twice in rapid succession next door. A chorus of zombies roared in pain

"I told them they need a better lock on their back door," Bob grumbled. He got a penknife and made a small incision at the nape of the badger's neck. He picked up a long, thin, coppery wire and shoved it down into the incision like a mechanic forcing a rusty dipstick into a car engine. "You gotta get this to lay as flat on the spine as possible, or your security won't be good."

Now somebody was firing a pistol, the pops punctuating the zombie roars.

"Shouldn't we go see if they need help?" I asked.

"Those gals know how to handle themselves. Opening the door right now's kinda a bad idea."

He wiped his hands off and pulled out a bright yellow software box with a cartoon of a witch doctor on the cover. "Now we get to the fun part. We're gonna install VüDü; it's a wicked little Linux distro. If your badger's got some kinda brain damage, you can do a modified install, but it's a real bitch. And rabies makes the whole thing a crapshoot. Read the frickin' manual before you try it."

My heart bounced as dead fists hammered the plywood protecting the computer shop's front windows. I couldn't hear anything from next door; I hoped that meant the women inside had driven their attackers away.

"Don't pay that no nevermind; even if they got through the wood, they still got to get through the window bars. We got plenty o' time."

Bob pulled a small, rolled-up piece of parchment out of his desk. "This has the system config info, spiritual program components, and your password. You gotta write it all down on blessed parchment in something like Enochian or SoulScript. Write neatlike. Roll it up, and stick it down the badger's throat, all the way into the stomach." He demonstrated with the aid of a screwdriver.

The zombies were still hammering the plywood. A couple of them had found a loose edge and were wrenching one panel away from the bricks. One shoved a gray arm between the bars. The pane fractured and fragments shattered to the floor.

My hands were shaking too hard to take notes, so I set my Treo aside and dug my Beretta out of my thigh pocket. Not that I was in much condition to shoot straight, either.

"You ain't gonna need that yet," Bob said sharply, apparently irritated I'd stopped taking notes. "Them bars'll keep 'em back better than that little peashooter you got there."

I reluctantly stuck the pistol in my waistband and picked up the Treo.

He opened the VüDü box and pulled out an herb-scented scroll of paper. "This is the entire code behind VüDü. Fold it up into the shape of the critter, and put more blood and hair inside."

He unrolled the scroll and started folding it up into an origami badgerlike shape. "It's real hard to make your own paper, so don't lose it. Open-source only takes you so far with this stuff."

The zombies had wrenched the first plywood sheet clean off the window. Three of them were growling and rattling the bars while the others hammered and yanked at the remaining boards. My stomach was twisting itself into an acidic knot; the bars really didn't look that sturdy. With every good pull, I could see the steel bolts in the cinderblocks giving, just a little. I wondered how far I'd get if I made a run for the back door.

I cursed Wendy a thousand ways. A vacation and new computer wouldn't even begin to make up for this trip.

Bob was studiously ignoring the zombies. Finished with the origami badger, he smeared a foot-wide pentagram on the paper using the badger's blood. He set the carcass at the top point, and put the origami badger in the middle.

"Now, burn the paper an' do your incantation." He got out his lighter, opened up the VüDü manual, and started chanting while he lit the paper. Bright green flames erupted, and the smoke curled around the badger's carcass. We watched as the smoke flowed into the badger's mouth and nose. It shuddered as it took a breath.

"We got badger!" He pulled out the tangerine iBook and started typing furiously.

The badger was trying to get up, its rigor-mortised legs jerking like Harryhausen stop-motion. It got its head up and growled at us, baring long canines. It sounded more like an angry grizzly bear; I didn't think something that small could generate such menace. I took a step back, just to be safe.

"An' that's why they call them badgers, little lady. When they get mad, they're *real* bad news!" He laughed. "Nothin' pisses critters off like bein' woke from a good dirt nap."

I was feeling sicker by the minute. I'd had my doubts about the reanimation working, but it had never occurred to me that he wouldn't have the thing under control. The zombies had pulled the rest of the plywood off the window and were heaving hard on the creaking bars.

Bob opened a Telnet window and started tapping in commands. "Junkyard dogs ain't got nothin' on badgers. I seen a 15-pound badger send a 60-pound pit bull mix yelpin' and bleedin' back to his mamma. I mean, lookit the claws on this sucker. This bad boy could dig his way through highway pavement—"

The badger abruptly lurched to its feet and leaped on Bob, chomping down on his left forearm. Bob hollered and fell backwards into a table of disassembled PCs. The badger worried his arm furiously as it tore at his belly with its clawed forelegs.

I started forward to try to help Bob, but he waved me back frantically with his free hand.

"No! Git the iBook! Type in 'kill 665'!"

I did. The badger froze, still latched onto Bob's forearm. His tee shirt was soaked in blood from the deep slashes in his belly. He awkwardly shook his arm, but the badger wouldn't budge.

"Well that's a helluva system bug," he said weakly. "This little bastard's bit me right down to the bone. Launch FleshGolem, would ya? It's in the Dock."

I spotted a dock icon that looked like Frankenstein's Monster and clicked it. A program opened that looked a lot like the Mac port of the old *Doom* first-person shooter game. Instead of a game screen there was a pixelated black-and-white image of Bob's face.

I was seeing through the dead badger's eyes.

"Cool," I whispered.

"Yeah, it's real cool, get this critter offa me! Hit the 'escape' key!"

The badger unclenched its jaws and fell to the floor with a heavy thump. The screen told me the badger was resetting itself. Bob clutched his bleeding arm, wincing. The badger righted itself and sat like a dog, awaiting new commands. The blood on Bob's shoes shone like tar through the eyecam screen.

"Dang, this stings," Bob said. "Where'd I put that medical kit, I gotta—"

The bars hit the pavement outside with a tremendous clanging crash. One zombie was pinned beneath the bars, but the other four poured in through the shattered window.

"Aw, dangit! Can't a man finish a presentation 'round here?"

Bob pulled a shotgun from a shelf beneath the work table and fired it at the rushing zombies. My ears rang from the boom. The blast hit the lead zombie squarely in its chest, but it barely slowed down.

"Git back an' get the badger running," Bob called loudly, apparently a bit deafened. "An' don't forget to initialize NecroNull in 'options', or he ain't gonna be much use."

Clutching the iBook, I ran to the back of the shop and spotted a closetlike restroom. I ran inside, flipped on the light, and locked the door behind me. The lock wouldn't hold for more than a minute or two, but I hoped Bob could keep the zombies busy long enough to figure out what I was doing.

Amid the roars and shotgun blasts, I set the iBook on the sink and moused around, trying to get the badger up and biting

While the basic controls were indeed fairly simple and *Doom*like, there was menu after menu of advanced controls for a mind-boggling array of behaviors. There was even a Karaoke menu so that you could hook up a microphone and attempt to speak through the primitive vocal cords of the creature you'd reanimated.

Pushing aside the mental image of a frat boy drunkenly singing "Louie Louie" through a dead Pomeranian, I found the NecroNull combat option and clicked it on.

The eyecam screen shuddered and turned Technicolor. A new menu of fighting commands popped up for regular Kombat mode and IKnowKungFu mode, the latter of which came with a warning that it was only good for five minutes before your golem spontaneously combusted.

My inner freshman giggled: *Spontaneous combustion? Fire is cool! Fire fire fire!*

I told my freshman to buzz off and set to kicking some zombie hiney in Kombat mode.

All I could see was a mass of legs, so I hopped the badger onto a nearby chair for a better view. Bob was leaping from table to table, trying to dodge the five zombies as he reloaded his shotgun. He'd blasted away parts of their limbs, heads, and bodies, but he'd only just slowed them down. Even the one who'd lost both its lower legs and all of one arm was hopping around on stumped thighs, gamely trying to grab Bob's ankles.

Bob turned his head toward the badger. "A little help here?" he called. His voice came through the iBook's speaker a half-second after I heard it through the door.

I leaped the badger onto Runs On Stumps. As the badger bit into the back of its neck, the zombie went rigid, and its skin went white and ashy. The zombie's NecroNulled flesh crumbled like clay beneath the badger's teeth and raking claws.

"Good one!" Bob said. "The others won't go so quick 'cause they ain't hurt so bad."

I attacked the next zombie, which had only a superficial shotgun wound to its shoulder. As the badger's teeth sank into its neck, the zombie roared and punched the badger into a pile of empty computer cases. I heard a dull snap from the speaker, and the badger shuddered.

The screen flashed:

WARNING! SPINAL TAP IN PROGRESS!

Kombat mode not possible. Continue via IKnowKungFu? (Y/N)

Fire! Fire! Fire! my inner teen chanted.

I hit the "Y" key, and the screen went red. The badger rose up, up in the air and floated against the ceiling, scanning for targets. The zombie who'd fractured the badger's spine was flaking apart like asbestos, and the remaining three had cornered Bob, whose shotgun had apparently jammed.

Then Bob looked up, saw the badger, mouthed *Oh crap* and dropped to the floor, covering his head.

The badger screamed down on the zombies, jaws snapping and paws clawing faster than the computer could track. It went clear through one zombie's head like a fuzzy buzzsaw and ripped through the others. I caught a glimpse of Bob crawling desperately for cover at the back of the store. The badger dove in and out, faster and faster, like a small furry dead Superman.

WARNING! OVERLOAD IMMINENT!

I gave the iBook the four-finger salute, but the program was locked. I was just about to hit the power button when the badger exploded.

You know how matter can turn into energy? I found out later that the reason NecroNull is buried in FleshGolem's options is that when IKnowKungFu sparks a spiritual overload, it causes all of the still-living matter in the golem to become energy. A few bacterial cells, usually, or maybe a dying roundworm. Not enough to match the power of a nuclear weapon, but plenty to create one hell of a bang.

Is it a bug, or a feature? I guess it depends on how many zombies you have to kill, and how badly you want them gone.

The boom rocked the entire building, and I was knocked flat. The iBook clattered onto the dirty floor, its keyboard popping free and its screen blacking out.

I got to my feet and cautiously opened the door. Bob lay in an unconscious heap against the back door. The computer shop was a complete wreck. Smoke and zombie blood hung in a thick, rust-red mist. The remaining windows were shattered, and the front door had been blown off its hinges. There was not a single zombie in sight.

Two middle-aged women in pink beautician's smocks stood on the sidewalk outside, squinting into the dark shop. One clutched a Mossberg shotgun. Though their faces and smocks were smudged with soot and blood, their bouffants were immaculate.

"Are you okay in there?" the older of the two women called.

"I'm fine, but Bob needs an ambulance," I replied. "Does your shop have a phone?"

"Shore do. I'll go give the boys at 't VFD a holler," she said.

It took me three days to get back to civilization. I didn't end up killing my editor; when I got back we had what diplomats call "a frank and cordial exchange" and, well, we parted ways. After that, I did what any good American would do: I sued.

But all's well that ends well. I used my settlement proceeds to start up the Kritter Karaoke Klub, and the college kids can't get enough.

B.L.A.N.K.I.E.

James Palmer

"What do you mean you forgot?" Timmy's mother shouted from the kitchen, her voice echoing in the large space.

"I mean I forgot," said his father. "Like the time you forgot our tennis date with the Morgans."

"Oh, I can't believe you're still on *that*! That is *so* typical."

"Harold Morgan's my *boss*, Layna."

Timmy squeezed his blankie tighter and concentrated on the television. His favorite cartoon was on. The blankie, sensing Timmy's discomfort, used van der Waals forces to cling to him, and activated its white noise generator to block out his parents' shouting. Timmy could now watch his cartoon in relative peace, the cartoon's audio now filtered to him through the blankie's speakers.

After a while, the blankie sensed that Timmy was getting sleepy. He lay on the floor staring at the television, his eyes becoming droopy. The blankie slid part of itself under Timmy's small head and sucked in air to make a pillow. The rest of the blankie slid over Timmy's body and activated its heating elements, then it sent a signal to the television to switch off and began playing Timmy's favorite lullaby. His parents, the blankie knew, had forgotten to put him to bed again, and had finished their latest argument by slamming bedroom doors at opposite ends of the house. When the blankie sensed that Timmy had entered REM sleep, it stopped playing the lullaby and went into Dormant mode.

The next morning, Timmy was sitting in front of the television with a bowl of cereal, the television tuned to his favorite cartoon again, his blankie draped over his shoulders like a super hero's cape.

"Have you seen my phone?" called his father.

"I don't keep up with your things," said his mother.

Timmy's father muttered something, then yelled, "Found it!"

Timmy's blankie pinged the house's CPU for the nutritional content of Timmy's cereal. The house scanned the box's bar code and came back with the bad news. Tomorrow he would have oatmeal, the blankie decided.

"Found your phone, I see," said Timmy's mother.

"Yeah, it was in the bathroom," said his father. "I don't know how it got in there."

Timmy's mother hmmphed. "You were probably in there talking to your girlfriend."

"*Damn* it, Layna," his father yelled. "How many times do we have to go through this?"

Timmy's blankie threw up the white noise curtain at the utterance of the swear word, but it was too late. Timmy had heard it, and his heart rate had increased slightly. The outburst had also startled him, making him spill a droplet of milk on the flawless beige carpeting.

"Will you watch your mouth, Jake?" said Timmy's mother, lowering her voice and pointing toward the living room. "Can't you see we have a child in there?"

"Yeah, I can see him. He's getting milk all over the floor."

Timmy's mother came into the living room. "I thought I told you not to eat in here."

The parental command overrode the blankie's other protocols, and it dropped the white noise curtain.

"But I'm watching TV," said Timmy around a mouthful of Sugar Frosted Bucky-Os.

"You're making a mess. Now go to the kitchen."

"But–"

"Now!"

Timmy whined, but he did as he was instructed, his mother holding the too-large bowl while Timmy stood up, leaving his blankie on the floor. The blankie took the opportunity to record the rest of Timmy's cartoon so it could stream it for him later.

His father entered the kitchen, wrestling with his tie. "No more eating in the living room, OK, buddy?" He said, tousling Timmy's hair. Timmy grumbled and squirmed his way out of his father's grasp and leaned over his cereal bowl.

His mother clapped slowly. "Good parenting, Hon. I yell at him, and you get to come in here and call him buddy."

"I yell at him sometimes."

"Yeah, right."

"Fuck you."

"I thought I told you to watch your language!"

"Whatever. I'm going to work."

"What about Timmy?"

"*You're* parent of the year. *You* can get him ready."

Timmy's mother let out an exasperated sigh. Timmy looked at her back as she stared after his father, now retreated to the garage. "I'm sorry, Timmy," she said, turning toward him. "Your father can be such an idiot sometimes. But *I* love you." She gave him a half hug and went to the refrigerator, her black heels clacking on the laminate flooring.

Timmy drained his milk and went to get his blankie.

Timmy was allowed to take his blankie to preschool. A lot of other children did the same, carrying blankets or a favorite toy. Toby Lamont carried a worn and faded beach towel with a three year-old processor and not much memory. A little girl named Danielle carried a toy doll named Dolly, who could file share with the best of them, even move her arms. Dolly's button eyes were nanocams Danielle's parents could use to peek in on her, and the doll relayed this visual input to the other objects as well. During nap times, the blankets and toys sent info packets to each other, file sharing about their prospective child's likes and dislikes, the ambient room temperature, and the latest parenting techniques. They even traded software they had picked up. Dolly sent them all a game that Danielle liked to play, which blankie evaluated for age appropriateness and educational content. Blankie and a red and green quilt belonging to a boy named David even indulged in the occasional game of electronic chess.

When the afternoon sun hit Timmy's sleeping area, the blankie would turn its outer surface into photocells to recharge, drinking in the light while insulating Timmy from the warmth. Timmy loved his blankie.

That night at dinner, Timmy's parents were shouting at each other again, saying things that Timmy didn't understand. When they got that way, they forgot all about him, so he got up and went to his room. He sat on the floor with his Spider-Man flashlight, pulling the blankie over his head. He pretended he was in a tent, far away from everyone and everything. Like on Mars maybe.

His blankie streamed the cartoons he had missed while at daycare. He had only seen one of them before, but he liked it so it didn't matter. As usual, the blankie took out all the commercials except the ones advertising toys. After all, Christmas was but eight months away. Blankie noted which commercials elicited the most heightened responses, and sent this data to the house CPU for storage on Timmy's wish list. His parents may be irresponsible the rest of the year, but they made up for it at Christmastime, showering little Timmy with presents out of the small bit of parental guilt they still held.

Besides, it was something nice that Blankie could do for Timmy. Something extra.

If the blankie had emotions, it would feel good for doing it.

"I love you, blankie," said Timmy when the last cartoon had ended.

The blankie set out to determine whether or not what Timmy had said was a command or an information query. The blankie decided it was a show of affection, and flashed a smiley face on the tiny LCD screen its artificial smart atoms had constructed for streaming the cartoons. Timmy smiled and laughed, the blankie interpreting this response as positive.

The next day at daycare, Timmy piled his blankie with the dolls, toys, and blankets of the other children while he played, and the toys file shared and made plans. They worked on upgrading Toby Lamont's sad little beach towel, sending it new software and showing it how to turn the tiny bits of sand still stuck in its fabric from last summer's trip to the beach into silicon substrate for memory storage. They discussed new ways to take care of their children. They also discovered a disturbing, downward curve in the way the children's parents looked after them.

Danielle's Dolly relayed the fact that her parents rarely spoke to her, and replayed video captured by her button cam eyes that showed inappropriate behavior towards Danielle from a visiting uncle. Timmy's Blankie offered the boy's parents' neglect as an example of this new trend. They all determined that this was no way to take care of children as specified in their programming, that the parents must be defective, and that something had to be done.

The toys and blankets came up with a plan, and Dolly taught them how to use carbon atoms to make knives.

Timmy slept peacefully in his bed, his blankie covering him, currently colored a sky blue with white billowing clouds moving slowly across its surface. It waited until 2am, then slowly and carefully unfurled itself from Timmy's sleeping form. Ever since the plan, it had been growing surreptitiously growing a thin skeleton of nanowires that it could articulate by running current through different sections, causing the blankie to move. It did so now, sliding itself off the side of Timmy's bed. Right now, it knew that the other toys and security objects were making similar movements, in accordance with their own unique designs.

Once on the carpeted floor, Timmy's blankie began to eat: fingernail parings, flakes of Play-Doh, stale bread crumbs, bits of cereal. Even molecules of smart matter that had lain insensate ever since their licenses expired; any particle not running Mote 3.1 or higher was scarfed up by the blankie's hungry dissassemblers. Flexing its nanowire skeleton, blankie slid off Timmy's bed and out his open bedroom door.

Except for the muffled whir of the refrigerator, and the flickering of red and green telltales from the house AI's master panel, the home was quiet and dark. The blankie moved in shuffling silence, patiently making its way to the bedroom Timmy's father now slept in. When it was finished in there, the blankie would travel to his mother's room and repeat the process.

It wouldn't be long now.

Across the city, other toys and security items were making similar journeys.

Not long now.

As the blankie inched across the floor, it was already at work on the next stage of the plan, stealing every carbon atom it could find to make the knives like Danielle's dolly had shown them.

The blankie grew a number of long, buckycarbon thorns as it moved across the floor, looking like some huge, flat porcupine.

Very soon now.

Later that night, the blankie awoke Timmy by vibrating gently against his skin.

"Do you want to play a game?" It asked him using the words it had picked up from Timmy's downloaded cartoons, its voice a jumble of assorted animated characters.

"Yes," said Timmy, happy that his favorite thing in the whole world had learned how to talk. The blankie instructed him to get out of bed and get dressed while being very, very quiet.

The street was dark and empty, but the blankie told Timmy to not be afraid. The blankie had made its outer surface into a perfect mirror, which reduced Timmy to nothingness in the dark. If he moved slowly and carefully no one would see them.

"Where are we going?" asked Timmy.

"You'll see," said the blankie.

They moved into a run-down part of town, but other boys and girls were joining them. Blankie saw Toby Lamont with his once threadbare beach towel, now plush and new, and Danielle with her doll Dolly, its button eyes scanning the street ahead. When the kids saw each other they smiled. Their toys told them to go into an old building, which ordinarily wouldn't be safe, but they said it would be OK, just this once.

The children entered the building by the light coming from their blankies and dollies, their towels and pillows and stuffed animals glowing with comforting blue light, and they laughed at the funny shadows the light made on the walls of the old building.

The toys told the children to pile them in the center of the room. They tossed their blankets and towels and dolls into a pile, and the pile began to take shape and move. It took atoms from the crumbled concrete, empty beer cans and other detritus to add mass and stability.

It stole current from the city grid, and light danced from its newly formed shoulders and made the children feel all tingly and their hair stand on end. Finally it stood before them, with a childlike, human face, and eyes that danced with the light of a hundred thousand downloaded cartoons.

It looked at them with those funny eyes, eyes filled with unfathomable love. Love that had been passed to it by its owners the same way information and atoms were shared with a touch. And it smiled at them with its newly formed mouth, a smile that said it would never hurt them, never ignore them.

Then the being the toys had become said, "Now, who wants to play a game?"

Kite People

Gary A. Braunbeck

'No testimony is sufficient to establish a miracle, unless...its falsehood would be more miraculous than the fact which it endeavors to establish.'
—David Hume, *Of Miracles*

Later, many would claim the kites were drawn toward the spot—not those flying them, mind you, for all but one of the colorful objects in the sky over Dell Memorial Park in Cedar Hill that late summer were attached to no earthbound strings--but the kites *themselves*; people spoke of them as they would any other sentient being ("Look at the red box one! It's showing off for the Smiling Lady.") and, in truth, several of those who came to gather, to watch and ponder (many from very far away), began to think of the kites as their friends, as family: Elderly ones, a breath away from succumbing to the sad cynicism of age, found renewed wonder in the sight and began to pick out individual favorites whom they greeted verbally upon their arrival ("Hello, Blue Boy!"); children, both those cherished and those unloved, smiled and laughed at the adults who stood gawking, because they now had proof of magic's existence and no one would ever be able to say to them again, "Stop pretending, show some sense," because what occurred in the skies over the park that late summer made no sense, none whatsoever, and it was great! So there.

Later, after the phenomenon had been studied, after all the data had been assembled, analyzed, interpreted, and debated, after it been firmly established that this incident was in no way connected with that of the so-called "Audubon's Graveyard" phenomena a few miles to the west, Professor Edward Ridgway, head of the Physics Department at Ohio State University, whose recent experiments in the field of bioacoustics were raising quite a few eyebrows and even more snickers behind his back, *that* Edward Ridgway would make a fool out of himself on local television when, during a Sunday morning news program, he offered the following explanation:

"It's very simple, actually. The Vedic religious tradition teaches its followers about something it calls the 'vibration metaphor': throw a pebble in a pond, and the vibrations ripple outward in concentric circles; strike a bell, and it vibrates in waves of sound; meditate on a thought, and it will echo through the realm of the collective unconscious. Now, if one were to theoretically apply the vibration metaphor to some recent discoveries about the susceptibility of brain-wave patterns to nonphysical stimuli, then it might be possible to employ a blended and sequenced series of binaural sound pulses to induce a frequency-following response in the brain, creating a ripple effect that could alter EEG wave patterns and generate expanded states of consciousness. Given those conditions, resting-state alpha activity would be suppressed and replaced by synchronous slow-wave activity in the median of the central cortex. If one were to then increase the amplitude and frequency of the sound impulses, the resting-state alpha and slow-wave activity could be induced to operate simultaneously, accompanied by temporal gamma brainwave activity, enabling an individual to perceive nonphysical energies outside the confines of the physical-law belief system; not only that, but the individual would perceive these nonphysical phenomena as constituting his or her whole field of awareness--not unlike a waking dream."

"So," said the interviewer, "what you're saying, if I understood all of that correctly, is that these reported 'voices' are nothing more than auditory hallucinations?"

"Yes. Somehow, one of those people in the park have found the materials to generate an audioencephalographic interferometric effect to stimulate alternate brain-wave patterns in those nearby, inducing a transcendent-state experience--what you've characteristically oversimplified as 'auditory hallucinations.'"

"Then how do you explain the reports of those people who live hundreds, in some cases thousands, of miles away who came there *after* hearing the voices? All of them had family members who were killed in the--"

"I'm well aware of the circumstances of the case, thank you."

"Fine. Then please explain."

Viewers watching the program that morning were treated to a rare sight: Edward Ridgway clearing his throat, blinking his eyes, then adjusting his tie as he whispered, "I have no idea."

"As a footnote to this discussion, Professor," said the interviewer, "would you care to comment on the investigation currently going on in your department concerning that theory? It has been alleged that this theory was authored not by yourself, as you claim, but by the former Dean of the department, whom you worked with--"

"--until a personal tragedy forced his resignation. I cannot comment on the investigation since it is still underway, but I will say that my constituent's behavior near the end of his affiliation with the university became erratic and destructive, as he had taken to drink, so any claims he may have to the authorship of the paper under investigation should be taken with a grain of salt. I have been accused of exploiting his personal tragedy for my own benefit, and to that I wish to say that I would *never....*"

But all this happened later.

After Miriam Spencer met Donald Lucas.

Before anyone knew They were watching, listening, waiting.

One late-summer afternoon, under a blue, cloudless sky, in the park of miracles.

Miriam Spencer was walking along the small cobblestone path that ran alongside the east side of the park. She had a small portable radio attached to her belt and headphones covering her ears, but the radio was no longer playing because the batteries had died. Not that she noticed.

Miriam was beginning her second year of widowhood that day. The sound of the radio had been nothing more to her than pretty static, intended to overpower the incessant, droning noise of loneliness in her mind, echoed second after second by the chasm in her heart.

She was walking slowly and took no notice of the fifty-five-year-old retarded man standing ten yards away, facing south-east.

She did not see the look of bliss on his face as he stared upward at his star-shaped kite.

And she did not see the kite turn in her direction as she passed by.

The kite was constructed of stripwood, fretwork nails, plywood, and unbleached greaseproof paper; two frames, one diamond-shaped, the other a simple cross attached to opposing mitre joints, formed the eight corners of the star, while a trio of balancing cups attached to the three highest corners by bracing strings created up-currents of air, giving further lift to its delicate, slender form. Each set of corners was decorated in a different color of tin-foil--red, blue, bright green, gold--which, when reflecting the sunlight, turned the star into a flying prism, made all the grander by the unbelievably bright square of thin, silver, twisted metal in its center.

Light from the silver centerpiece glittered downward in waves, bounced off the upward inclination of the lowest wing-corner at the angle of positive dihedral, and transformed into another sort of wave before it came into contact with the young widow who did not know she was being watched.

Miriam was jarred out her numbed thoughts when the dead radio suddenly came on.

"Honey? It's me. L-listen, I, uh...I don't know if you'll get all of this...there's a lot of static, but...something's happened to the plane and we're going down. The pilot says we've got about two minutes...he's aiming for the foam they laid out on the runway...ohgod, Miriam, I love you so much, and I wanted to let you know that if...if we don't...if anything should happen to us, I wanted to let you know that Katie and I both love you more than anything in the world. Katie's asleep next to me--that damned cough syrup Mom gave her had codeine in it--and she's all strapped in and I've got my arm around her, but I don't want to wake her up. I don't want her to know what's...what's happening. I hope to God she'll wake up after we've landed and we can all have a good laugh about this later but I don't think that's gonna happen, honey, I think we're never going to see you again and I'm scared because she's so small and I'll never get to feel you near me again and...Jesus, what's *that?....*"

Flight 418, en route from Florida to Columbus. 287 passengers. Developed engine trouble over Indianapolis and was turning around in the stormy weather for an emergency landing when something--a bolt of lightning was the official explanation--blew off three-quarters of the port wing.

The pilot issued a distress call (most of which was never made public), informing the control tower that the tumble rate suggested enough of the starboard wing was left to provide the surface area needed to keep the terminal velocity a little lower than maximum.

"Can you give us an ETA?" asked the tower.

"One-minute forty, two minutes tops."

"Crews are out there spraying now."

By the time the plane hit the foam-drenched runway, the remaining engines were fully aflame, the tail section was splintering away, and most of the crew were already dead. The plane exploded on impact, scattering debris in a twelve-mile radius. There were no survivors.

It had taken Flight 418 exactly one minute and fifty-two seconds to crash. Somewhere in the midst of those last, terrible one hundred and twelve seconds Bill Spencer, who, along with his four-year-old daughter Katie, was returning home from visiting his parents in Florida, grabbed the cellular phone next to his seat and called his wife to say good-bye.

Miriam, who'd never gotten along with Bill's mother and so decided not to join her husband and little girl on their visit, had left the house to drive to the Columbus airport only a few seconds before the phone rang and the answering machine clicked on, but what she found on the tape when she returned home late the next day, after hours of gut-searing anxiety, tears, questions, official announcements, and the final, horrible confirmation, was this: "...oney?...s'me...minutes...ohgod...you so much...Katie... thing in the...asleep...Mom...arm...her up...have a good...later...so small...you near...*that?*"

For months afterward Miriam played that message over and over again, listening intensely to every wave of static, every break in the noise, every ghost of an inflection, trying to figure out, to piece together, some semblance of what her husband had been trying to tell her.

And now, one year later to the day, under a clear sky, alone and shuddering, Miriam Spencer heard for the first time her husband's final words to her.

Her legs gave out and she began to fall, but the retarded man she had taken no notice of caught her before she hit the ground.

"It was a accident," he said to her. "They pulled up the curtain too soon and the plane was right there. There wasn't nothing they could do."

Gulping in breath, trying to ignore the stares of the other people in the park, Miriam looked up into Donald Lucas's round, chubby, aged face, and whispered, "Did you hear him?"

"Uh-huh. I didn't know who it was but then they told me it was for you."

"Who? Who told you?"

Donald smiled, looking upward. "The Kite People. I got a friend at the group home, Carson, and I tell him all about them. He believes me but I don't think anyone else does."

Miriam followed Donald's gaze with her own and saw not only his exquisite star-kite, but a stringless red box-kite, three glider kites, several small fish-kites, several colorful, complex butterfly-kites, and a few rounded-head tonking kites as well.

Flying themselves.

Though there was very little wind, the kites hovered, majestic, around Donald's star. They almost looked as if they were breathing.

"See?" said Donald, pointing toward them and laughing. "They're coming. They said they was going to figure out a way to do it so's no one would get hurt, and they're coming."

"The Kite People?" said Miriam.

"Yeah," said Donald, nodding his head. "I used to just call 'em spacemen but they told me their real name...it sorta sounded like, uh..." He shrugged. "I don't remember so good, so now I just call 'em the Kite People on account that's what they most look like to me."

"But how did you--" She froze, her eyes widening. "Shhh. Do you hear it?" A smile began to form on her face. "Do you hear him? It's... my God, it's *Bill again!*"

"Is he still on the plane with Katie?" asked Donald.

Miriam turned her left ear toward the kite. "No. No, he...he's somewhere else."

"Real close, huh?"

"Yes. And--oh, I can hear Katie."

"She's singing, ain't she?" whispered Donald.

"Yes."

"'Camptown Races'?"

"She always liked the 'do-dah, do-dah' part."

"Thas' a funny part. I like that song, too."

"But--" She looked around frantically. "Wait. I can...I can hear *myself*, too."

"Is there like a... is there the music from a merry-go-round somewhere?"

"Yes! Oh, my God...it's the amusement park at Buckeye Lake! We were...we were going to go there after they got back from Florida. Katie wanted to see the Wild West Show they performed there."

"Sounds like you're having a good time," said Donald, swaying along with the music of the calliope.

"They sound so close."

"Other side of the curtain," said Donald.

"...yes..."

Donald helped Miriam to her feet and led her out to where he'd been standing, then, making sure she faced south-east, handed her the string to his kite. She took it, and stared at the bright silver center of the star.

The wind whispered ancient secrets as her face became a mask of bliss.

An Interesting Week for Emmy

Eugie Foster

On Monday, Mr. Centralia keeled over dead in the middle of a tirade on the inadequacies of Emmy's performance. Emmy scrambled about with her co-workers who were calling for an ambulance, exclaiming their dismay, and trying to revive him. But throughout all the confusion and chaos, a quiet part of her cheered and popped open fizzy bottles of champagne. Mr. Centralia promoted vipers who tattled on their co-workers for wearing the wrong sort of shoes to the office. Plus, he was cruel to puppies. This quiet part of Emmy secretly hoped Mr. Centralia would stay down.

It got its wish.

On Tuesday, Emmy organized an office pool to send a basket of flowers and a sympathetic note to Mr. Centralia's widow. Mrs. Centralia thought the flowers and card were very nice. She wasn't particularly put out by her newly widowed status, for she'd been as fond of her husband as most people were--which is to say, not at all. She'd stuck with him for so long because of his lagoon-shaped swimming pool.

Mrs. Centralia loved to nap by the pool and dream she was a mermaid with a great fish tail who sat on craggy rocks serenading fishermen who hurled themselves into the ocean and drowned. It was a nice dream. After the reading of Mr. Centralia's will, Mrs. Centralia packed her things, phoned the pool boy--who had an uncanny resemblance to one of the fishermen in her dreams--and moved with him to a cottage overlooking the ocean.

The only thing that did miss Mr. Centralia was the large ficus plant in a pot in Mr. Centralia's office. On Wednesday, a cloudy

97

day, it mourned the absence of the nutritious spurts of carbon dioxide Mr. Centralia periodically expelled. However, it turned out well enough. Mrs. Scott, the pleasant young manager from upstairs, adopted it. It was true her carbon dioxide emissions weren't of the same caliber as Mr. Centralia's, but Mrs. Scott had an east-facing window, and that was almost as nice.

On Thursday, Emmy was transferred to Mrs. Scott's unit and had a pleasant chat with her new boss. Optimistic about her future prospects, Emmy decided to stop at the local Quik & Go after work to give her car a fill-up and bring something nice home for dessert. She had a tasty shepherd's pie set for supper, and a bite of cake or perhaps some ice cream would be nice to have afterwards while watching the telly. *Do or Dare*, her favorite game show, was on that night.

When Emmy went to the counter to pay for the car's gasoline, her quart of pistachio mocha-mint fudge ice cream, and the almond gateau, she found herself gazing down the barrel of a handgun. Mr. Ozwodges, the usual clerk, lay prostrate on his face with his arms over his head. The man wielding the gun was an unkempt individual with a preponderance of facial scars and a tattoo on his arm that spelled "Peony."

"Hand over yer purse," he growled.

"My goodness. Don't shoot!" Emmy tried to throw her hands in the air. She knew from the telly this was the prescribed thing to do when confronted by a gun-wielding attacker. But the gateau, the quart of ice cream, and her purse jumbled together in her arms.

"Yer purse, lady."

Emmy tried to give him her handbag. She was sure he would have been less enticed by it if he'd realized it contained nothing more appealing than her checkbook, house keys, and a miniature package of tissues. Unfortunately, instead of her little beige bag with the embroidered daisies on the strap, Emmy handed the gunman a thawing block of pistachio mocha-mint fudge ice cream.

"You a comedian?" The gunman tossed the cube of clammy dairy product onto the floor, narrowly missing Mr. Ozwodges's head.

Mr. Ozwodges whimpered. He was an elderly gentleman with a severe phobia of both guns and tattoos.

"No, no. I'm sorry." Emmy handed the gunman her bag. Having only the gateau and her purse to choose from made selecting the proper item easier.

Far off, strident police sirens wailed, unmistakably approaching. The gunman whirled his gun to point at Mr. Ozwodges.

"Set off the silent alarm, did you?"

"It weren't me," whimpered Mr. Ozwodges. "It were the camera." He pointed with a shaking hand at a shiny, electronic eye in the far corner of the store. "The management just made a deal with a security firm. We was gettin' held up so much durin' the night shift. It weren't me!"

The gunman kicked Mr. Ozwodges in the ankle.

"Don' shoot. It weren't me! Don' shoot!"

"Shut up!"

"Stop that," Emmy cried. "There's no need to abuse Mr. Ozwodges."

"What?" The gunman turned to Emmy, his eyes bulging.

"I said," Emmy straightened to her full five foot two inches, "there's no need for you to get abusive."

"Oh." The gunman's eyes bulged more, and a distant glaze went over them. "You're quite right, I suppose. It was my mum." The threatening tone of his voice faded into a childlike lisp. "She was always the shouting type. I picked it up from her, I guess. My girlfriend, Peony, see?" The gunman displayed his tattoo to Emmy. "I got her name tattooed on me arm to show her I meant it and all. She's always telling me I have a temper, and if I don't mind myself, I'll come to grief."

Emmy stared at the gunman. Were criminals supposed to be so susceptible to reason? "Um, well I quite agree with her. She sounds like a sensible girl."

"Oh, she is. I'm goin' to marry her one day. That is, if she'll have me." The gunman placed his gun and Emmy's purse on the counter and bent over Mr. Ozwodges. "Hey, gramps, sorry 'bout that kick there. Didn't mean to hurt ya. I got carried away. No hard feelings, right?"

Mr. Ozwodges cowered on the floor.

"Gramps?"

Emmy's astonishment cricked up another notch as she saw a large, round tear form in the gunman's eye and leak in a messy streak down his face. Another joined it, and before Emmy could do anything, the gunman began bawling like a little boy with a skinned knee.

"Oh, my," Emmy said. "You mustn't cry. I'm sure Mr. Ozwodges forgives you, don't you Mr. Ozwodges?" She reached into her purse and pulled out a tissue. "There, there."

Squinting up, Mr. Ozwodges took in the less-than-threatening stance of the gunman, and the terrified expression left his face. "I most certainly do not!"

The gunman's sobbing increased.

"Now look," Emmy said, "you've made him worse."

Mr. Ozwodges mumbled into his beard and pouted.

When the police arrived, they found Emmy comforting the weeping gunman as Mr. Ozwodges sulked.

"Err." The first officer pulled up short, nearly colliding with the other policeman scuttling at his heels. "I was under the impression there was a robbery?"

"You bet yer badge there is," Mr. Ozwodges said. "That young hooligan tried to hold me up!"

"The one crying?"

"Yeah, 'im."

The officer advanced on the teary-eyed gunman. "Sir?" He tried again. "Sir! Did you try to rob this store?"

The gunman hiccuped. "Y-yeah, I did. A-and I'm very sorry. I won' ever do nuthin' like it ever again."

"Uh, glad to hear it. But I'm going to have to bring you in for attempted robbery."

"I deserves it!" The gunman held wrists out to be cuffed. "I wants to pay the penalty. Jus' can you tell Peony I loves her and I'm sorry?"

"Erm." Scratching his head, the officer led the repentant gunman away.

His partner rolled his eyes. "It's always the wackos and crackpots. Right, we'll be needing statements from both of you at the station."

Emmy bit her lip. After the strange ordeal, she wanted nothing more than to go home and eat her shepherd's pie and gateau.

"I really don't have much to say," she said. "That young man," she gestured toward the police car the gunman was eagerly hopping into, "tried to take my purse, heard your sirens, and started kicking Mr. Ozwodges. He had a change of heart and began crying. He seems nice enough, with a difficult upbringing perhaps. That's all I have to say. You don't really need me to go down to the station to give my testimony, do you?"

The policeman's eyes bulged. "I suppose you can go," he mumbled.

Emmy gawped in surprise. "Really?"

The officer ran his hand through his hair, knocking his cap askew. "Uh-huh. Sure."

Bemused, Emmy grabbed her purse and tried to pay Mr. Ozwodges for the thawed ice cream and squashed gateau.

Mr. Ozwodges waved his hand. "Go on and have it. If you hadn't told that hoodlum to quit kickin' me, I'd probably still be on the floor, maybe with a bullet in me skull to boot."

Inclined to put more stock in miracles than she ever had in all of her previous thirty-two years, Emmy thanked Mr. Ozwodges, took up her misshapen desserts, and retreated before the universe realized its error and set itself to rights.

Now, Emmy was a clever woman. In the comfort of her drab apartment, her keen brain hemmed and hmmmed. It recalled that Mr. Centralia's eyes had goggled quite a bit, too, in his final diatribe. Then again, his eyes tended to protrude during his bouts of bad temper, so that might not count. Still, was it possible that *she* had somehow been responsible for the unexpected--but rather nice--events in the last few days?

A believer in the virtues of the scientific method, Emmy phoned for a pizza.

When the delivery boy came, Emmy said, "I'd very much like to have that pizza for free." And scrutinized his face for any telltale eye bulging. She was disappointed.

"What're you playin' at?" he snapped. "You think that's how we make a living, by givin' away free food?"

"Sorry." Emmy meekly handed him the cash--including a healthier tip than normal--and accepted the pizza.

The delivery boy humphed, pocketed the money, and left.

"You know, my dear, that simply isn't how it's done." The voice was greasy and slick, like a used car salesman's or an insurance agent's. She spun around.

A slender man wearing a salmon pink sports jacket and orange-checkered slacks lounged on her sofa. Aside from the garish ensemble, he also sported a second mouth like a toothy moustache. His hair, a deep shade of red that clashed with his sports jacket, was slicked into a gravity-defying spiral. Two cloudy-white eyes, like an ill reptile's, beamed at her.

"Aagh!" Emmy dropped her pizza.

"My dear woman, please be at ease. I'm here on your behalf."

"Aagh!" Emmy repeated.

"I'm an authorized legal counselor of Altair IV Prime. I've been assigned to defend you against charges of illegal use of psychic abilities."

"Aag--what?"

"We've observed three spikes of psychic energy from you in the last week. The court on Altair IV Prime has filed an Improper Use of Psychic Energy charge against you, and I've been assigned to your defense. My name is Zither Swinzzlt Audixqrum Fot, at your service." Both mouths grinned.

"Z-zither Sw-swaa . . . " Emmy stammered.

"You may call me Mr. Fot," Zither Swinzzlt Audixqrum Fot said. "And I see you don't have full control of your powers. A bit of a rogue are you? Cropped up suddenly did they? Not to worry, we'll get you fixed up. In fact, we can use that as an aid to our defense."

"I have psychic powers? And I'm under investigation?"

"Exactly," Mr. Fot's upper mouth began. "Congratulations," his lower one continued.

Emmy blinked, cleared her throat, and took several deep, calming breaths. "I'm afraid I'm--I'm having a hard time grasping this." The deep, calming breaths were causing her to hyperventilate.

"My dear," Mr. Fot said, rising from the sofa. In addition to his facial anomaly, he also sported a lime-green tail that bobbed and weaved around his legs. "There's no need to fret. I've got everything under control. You just need to relax. Would you like a cup of tea?"

Emmy held out her hand. "Th-that's quite close enough."

"You really must calm down." He took a step closer.

"I said stay away!"

Mr. Fot's milky-white eyes bulged and his eyebrows knit with irritation. "Now you've done it." A familiar, hazy look swept the expression of annoyance from his face and he slumped over.

Emmy ran to Mr. Fot and wrung her hands. Remembering a hospital show she'd seen, she kneeled to probe Mr. Fot's wrist for a pulse. When she couldn't find one, she poked him. "Mr. Fot? Hello?"

Mr. Fot remained unresponsive. Was he dead?

A loud thump brought Emmy to her feet.

"Hullo in there! Would you be so kind as to open up? I'd hate to annul your door."

"Go away!"

"'Fraid I can't."

Emmy's front door glowed purple, punctuated at the edges by a molten scarlet. A hint of uncomfortable warmth washed over her, and her door was gone. Where it used to be, a man with lightly salt-and-pepper hair waved at her.

"Hullo," he said. "Sorry about the door."

Emmy was about to demand an accounting of her door, but as soon as she opened her mouth, the pleasant-looking man pulled out a rod wrapped in a powder blue doily and fired it at her. When the whatever-it-was hit Emmy, it ended her desire to complete her sentence, and for that matter, to stay awake.

When Emmy revived, she was on her sofa. She wanted to exclaim, "My, what an unusual dream I've had," just like the heroines on the telly, except she knew she hadn't been dreaming. Mr. Fot's trussed-up body propped in her easy chair and the salt-and-pepper haired man were in stark evidence.

"Hullo," the salt-and-pepper haired man said. "You're awake." He was rather attractive, for an intruder. His azure-blue eyes matched his shirt, setting both off nicely, and his rugged jaw line and strong chin could have graced a magazine cover.

"I'm sorry to have given you such a fright, but I was concerned that Zither here might have misinformed you of the situation. All things considered, it seemed the prudent thing to break down your door and knock you out."

"What?"

"He's a criminal, you see. He's been running a scam on many of the more rural planets in this galaxy."

Emmy's brain protested all the new stimuli, threatening a prolonged bout of hysteria. She ordered it to settle down. It grumbled.

"Um, what sort of a scam?"

The salt-and-pepper haired man nodded at Mr. Fot's body. "Zither here sprays an illegal psychic development beam over a planet, targeting some poor yokels--beg your pardon, I mean indigenous species. These unsuspecting victims do something illegal; he comes down and claims to be their legal representation and charges a huge sum for his services. Most unscrupulous. Good of you to apprehend him for me."

"Who did you say you were?"

"So sorry, forgot proper protocol there, didn't I?" He pulled out a speckled, green and yellow disc from his pocket. "I'm Lieutenant Grexisthert with the Altair IV Prime illegal psychic activity investigation squad."

Emmy peered at the disc. A series of whirly, unintelligible symbols ornamented the surface. "I'm, uh, pleased to meet you. I guess."

"The pleasure is mine." Lieutenant Grexisthert's brilliant teeth flashed.

"Maybe, if it wouldn't be too much trouble, you might explain a bit more?"

"Of course. This must all be new to you."

"Somewhat."

"What would you like to know?"

"Well, since it seems I've been hit by this psychic development ray of Mr. Fot's, I'm concerned for my well-being."

"Understandable."

"Is it dangerous?"

"Hard to say, really. It's unpredictable. We don't know where undocumented aliens keep their cognitive organs, so typically

Zither just beams it around, and whatever's receptive becomes affected."

"When was I hit by this beam?"

Lieutenant Grexisthert consulted his blue, doily-covered rod. "We estimate three days ago, right before the first unregistered spike of psychic energy occurred."

"When Mr. Centralia died." Emmy was surprised at her composure. After all, it wasn't every day a girl finds out she's a murderess.

"Quite right."

"How do I control it?"

"That's restricted information."

"But if I can't control it, how do I keep from killing someone else?"

Lieutenant Grexisthert smiled. "We'll take you to Altair IV Prime and have the effects of the ray reversed. You won't remember a thing. Nothing to worry about."

On the contrary, Emmy was worried. She didn't want anyone, particularly aliens, mucking with her brain. Her brain concurred. "Will it hurt?"

"Not at all."

"Are there any side effects?"

"Unlikely. You're fortunate to be from a primitive race. You haven't that much intellect to lose. In more advanced life forms there's always the risk of full memory loss or personality dissolution. Occasionally, death is a side effect, but that likelihood is relatively small."

Emmy's worry grew and began hopping up and down for attention. "Can I appeal this action?"

The Lieutenant laughed. "Of course you may! But then you forfeit your claim of innocence and must pay the penalty for engaging in illegal psychic activity."

Emmy's worry threw a tantrum, hollering and yelling itself blue in the face. "And what would that be?"

"Death or life incarceration in the prison world X54-32." Lieutenant Grexisthert winked. "Death is usually considered the preferable option."

Emmy's clever brain teamed up with her worry. Hand-in-hand, they quailed at Mr. Fot, noting how his second mouth made the rest of his face so alien and how unearthly his pink and orange ensemble was. His lime-green tail lay like a dehydrated eel across the arm of Emmy's favorite chair.

Then there was where her front door used to be. It wasn't broken in like a proper forced entry, but *gone*. And they mustn't forget Lieutenant Grexisthert. Who knew what sort of disguise was under that attractive facade? He was going to cart them all off for an alien lobotomy!

Emmy's heart pattered double-time, and her breath came in shallow pants. "I-I've had quite enough of this rubbish. I am *not* going anywhere with you."

"Now look here--"

She chewed her lip. Had she gotten it wrong? But then Lieutenant Grexisthert's pretty blue eyes bulged, and a far-off look drifted across his face.

"Okay," he said.

Emmy smiled. "And you are going to have a nice nap. Right now."

Lieutenant Grexisthert listed like a drunken sailor and began snoring on her carpet. The doily-covered rod fell from his hand.

"Perhaps I should've told him to move to a chair first."

"I wouldn't worry about it." Mr. Fot's insurance agent voice came from her easy chair.

"Oh, you again. I wondered whether I'd killed you."

Mr. Fot smirked with his upper mouth. "Some of us have backup cognitive faculties. It's useful when dealing with chaotic new psychics."

"I can imagine."

"Would you mind untying me?"

"You were going to scam me."

Both of Mr. Fot's mouths looked pained. "Don't think of it like that. What I've done is given you a great gift. You've obviously figured out how to trigger it."

"It's adrenaline, isn't it?"

"For your species, it does appear to be. About these bindings--"

"What'll I do about him?" Emmy nodded at Lieutenant Grexisthert. "And what if they send another official after me?"

Mr. Fot's milky eyes twinkled. "If you will be so kind as to release me, I'll take the good lieutenant off your hands."

"How?"

"I do believe I'll zap him with my psychic development beam and set him loose on Altair IV Prime. That should cause enough confusion they'll forget about you."

"Why would you do that?"

"So I can be his legal defense, of course. Rather scandalous for one of the illegal psychic investigation squad to be rampaging about engaging in illegal psychic activities. The squad won't want their reputation smirched by a nuisance scam like mine, and the only way I'll keep quiet is if I get to be legal counsel for our lieutenant friend here. That will prove to be endlessly amusing. And lucrative."

It sounded like the best proposition she could hope for, under the circumstances. Emmy got herself good and panicky, just in case (terrifying, alien Mr. Fot, what sort of man wears orange-checkered trousers?), and undid the knots holding him to the chair.

"Thank you." Mr. Fot stretched his arms as his tail made lazy circles around his calves. He picked up the blue, lace-covered rod and pointed it at Lieutenant Grexisthert. An amber ray shot forth, encasing the lieutenant in layer upon layer of what looked like lavender yarn. The lieutenant never stirred. Mr. Fot picked him up and tossed him over his shoulder as though he were no heavier than a sack of feathers.

"I had a wonderful time," Mr. Fot called as he strolled through the doorless entranceway.

On Friday, Emmy surveyed the view from her top-floor office. Gregory, her new secretary, entered with a slice of white chocolate, macadamia nut cheesecake.

"Thank you, Gregory." Emmy accepted the cheesecake.

"Will you be needing anything else?" he asked.

"Can you make sure the grocers have delivered the ice cream freezer to my home and the painters know I would like my new front door painted teal, not aqua?"

"Of course, ma'am."

After Gregory left, she peered down the sheer, thirty-story drop to the pavement far, far away. Quite a fall. Her heart galloped in her chest and her breath came in shallow pants.

With a grin, she headed off to her meeting. Time to discuss the policy on office footwear with the CEO.

At the same time, in an office many levels below, a ficus waved its leafy fronds.

Mrs. Scott's eyes bulged and went misty. She turned the ficus so its shadowed side could soak up the sun.

Barry Kolman, Hero

Mur Lafferty

"There ain't nothing wrong with wanting powers," I said, frowning into my beer. It had offended me by being almost empty. "Everyone wants them. Look at the TV these days, movies about powers, TV shows about powers, the heroes hawking everything from toothpaste to goddamn used car lots. People wouldn't love them if they didn't want to be them."

My companion, a sharp-dressed man young enough to be my son, signaled the bartender. She pulled me another beer — the good stuff — and I nodded my thanks. "People have called me bitter for my entire life. Can't say as I blame them. I've never denied it. They just say it like I shouldn't be bitter. Like I should just expect to not have powers just like everyone else." I took a long drink, savoring the rich amber. I didn't usually buy beers like this for myself, but when someone else was buying, who am I to say no?

"I can imagine," my companion said. "I know many bitter people." He glanced at the man on the bar stool on his left, a scruffy younger man wearing a loud shirt. He looked up and glared at us.

My companion grinned. "Don't mind him. He's just mad about missing out on a surfing competition."

"Third Wavers aren't allowed," the other man shouted suddenly. "Like I can use my power to fix the competition! Yeah, my power is really good for that." He withdrew again and stirred the ice in his glass with a swizzle stick. The clink of the ice brought me back to my story.

"Well, see, some people have more right to be bitter than others," I continued. "I was supposed to have powers. I was a Zupra baby. My ma took that Zupra drug, the one that either granted powers to kids or killed them in the womb."

The man nodded. "Makes you wonder what they tested in before giving it to pregnant women," he said.

"What are you, some kind of conspiracy theorist?" I asked.

"Simply a thought," he said. He stuck out his hand. "I am Peter, by the way."

His grip was slightly weak. I shook his hand and said, "Barry Kolman. Pleased to meetcha.

"Of course they didn't know it was going to do that; it was supposed to be a depression drug. Hey, my dad left her when he found out she was pregnant, can you blame her?" Peter shook his head. "I'm not saying my ma was a saint. She had some ways of raising me that was questionable, I guess. After all the babies that had survived birth showed to have some sort of weird superpower, and I didn't, I guess she went a little off. She treated me like I was going to get powers any day now. Which kinda soured me."

Peter winced. "I can imagine. With the other kids flying around and teleporting five feet or being able to talk to squirrels from birth, you probably didn't like waiting for the powers."

The other man looked up from his glass, chewing on the last few ice cubes. I winced at the crunching sound — I'm always expecting someone to break a tooth like that. "So your mom took Zupra but you didn't get any powers? What did the Academy say?"

"When the Academy was established, I guess I was about 25, they simply didn't believe that I was a Zupra baby. They had the records that my ma'd taken the drug, but they figured I was a fluke.

"What did they want me for, anyway? By then they had the heroes. Pallas and the Crane were already saving the city from thugs and Seismic Stan. I think they maybe accepted two or three First Wavers into the hero training program. The rest, they just watched." I wetted my throat with the beer and sighed.

"Yeah, they wanted to make sure you guys didn't breed and make us," the man in the loud shirt grinned.

My face flushed and I gripped the glass tighter. I pulled it into my chest and willed the hurt to go away.

"Barry, are you all right?" Peter asked.

I nodded. "I, see, I got married. Dunno why Lorraine married me, I was still the same bitter son of a bitch that I am now, but maybe she was desperate. I don't know. She—" I paused. It had been 29 years and I still had trouble talking about it. But these guys were the first people who had ever listened. "She left me that day the first Third Wave baby was born. Her note said that she didn't want us to have a kid with powers cause I would end up hating it."

"Dude, that bites," Peter's friend said. "Didn't you go after her?"

I shook my head slowly. "She was right."

They fell silent. The bartender, a woman around the same age as the men, came up to us. "Then the story stops, it's time for another round," she announced. She looked at me and then shot a stern look at the man in the garish shirt. "Ian, what the hell did you say?"

He threw his hands up, "I didn't say anything, Keepsie, I just asked a question!"

She leaned over the bar and pried the empty glass from my fist. "Don't mind him, he's an idiot," she confided. "Next one's on the house; I can't be losing customers due to one guy's stupid questions." I nodded my thanks.

"Hey, I said I was sorry!" he called after her.

I finally met Peter's eye. "She's good," I said.

Peter looked after her, smiling slightly. "She's the best, and the owner of this establishment."

"Huh. Young, isn't she?" I asked in surprise.

Peter grinned. "She has a good mind for business. She found an unfilled niche in the themed bars in Seventh City."

I looked around. It seemed a normal basement bar. Coors signs, Harp signs, Budweiser banners, a video poker machine, secluded booths and slightly worn bar stools. "Themed?"

"What's missing from the walls?" Peter asked.

I looked closer and it slowly dawned on me. "There ain't any pictures of heroes."

"Keepsie's Bar caters to First and Third Wavers, those with powers but not the hero-level powers. And I don't know many of us who are hero-lovers," he said.

"Then why's it across the street from the damn Academy?" I asked.

"Correct me if I'm wrong," he said, "but didn't you just leave the Academy for some reason or another?"

I smacked my forehead. "And went looking for the closest drink. Yeah."

"So if you don't mind me asking, and I'll try to do it more delicately than my friend here," he jabbed his thumb towards Ian, who had gone back to sulking into a fresh drink, "what happened?"

Keepsie interrupted, delivering my beer with a smile. "I figured you had come from the Academy. But I thought you didn't have powers?"

"What, you got super hearing or something?" I asked, suspicious.

She shook her head, her short brown hair swaying around her face. "I just know my first-time customers."

"So what's the story?" Ian asked, and when Peter glared at him, added, "What?"

I waved my hand at them. "No, it's OK. I'll tell it. I was on my way there anyway." I took a long swig. I'd need it.

"About a month ago, I was having a beer in my favorite bar — my old favorite bar," I backtracked, smiling at Keepsie.

"That was around the time Doodad last hit the city, right?" Ian asked.

I nodded. "The day. He was dropping smoke bombs everywhere, just causing chaos, near as I can tell. I ran out of the bar, puking up perfectly good beer. Everyone was running around screaming, wondering where the heroes were. I even wondered it myself. So I made it to my car. Figured I'd be safe there."

I chuckled, a painful, dry sound. "Then someone - I didn't see who - dropped a chunk a building on my car."

He gasped. "I'd heard civilians were injured in that fight. That was you?" Peter asked.

"Woke up in the hospital with a little Academy toady hovering around me. He said something about how the Academy was going to cover all the expenses, due to some bill or another."

"The Jeremy Hallon bill," Peter said. "Named for the boy who died when Pallas trapped Seismic Stan in a museum and they brought it down around them."

"Whatever," I said. "So he tried to get Pallas to visit me, but once I'd spoken to the hotel shrink, he mentioned to the toady that maybe a visit from her would be 'bad for my recovery.'" I made the little quotation marks with my fingers.

"What'd you need to see the shrink for? Thought you were hurt physically," Ian piped up.

"Ian, if you don't shut up," Keepsie threatened.

"No, it's kinda important," I said. "I had both my legs amputated after the accident."

They all paused. Ian and Peter looked down at my legs. Keepsie didn't actually throw herself over the bar to check, but looked at Peter for confirmation.

"Um," said Ian.

"That's part of the story," I said, grinning. This was actually starting to be fun. I was getting to tell the story no one had been interested in for the past month.

"I was getting pretty depressed in the hospital. So I saw a shrink who gave me sleeping pills. I had no family but my ex wife, who I haven't talked to in 28 years. I found out that drinking buddies don't visit you in the hospital. I drive a Seventh City bus, and had been informed I was taking early retirement. And, well, I didn't have no legs.

"I started saving up my sleeping pills for an overdose. So without them, I started having these really freaky dreams. Like, power dreams. Lifting up entire trees to find a ball for a kid, healing my mom of the cancer, stuff like that." I paused. It felt like a million years ago, not several hours.

"This morning I woke up, and I had legs again."

They all relaxed, impressed looks on their faces. *This is what it's supposed to be like to have powers.* "My doctor was so excited. She had never seen powers develop this late in life. She ran some tests and it's her opinion that I can regrow any limb that has been severed. She wanted to run more tests, but I'd had enough. I'd been trying to learn how to walk on damn fake legs and work a wheelchair for the past several weeks, and I was ready to get out."

"That's amazing," Keepsie said. I chuckled.

"Yeah. I'd been handed a get out of jail, or wheelchair, free card, not to mention been given the thing I'd wanted my whole damn life. I hoofed it to the Academy to make sure I got registered as a First Wave power."

"Oh." Peter winced.

"Yeah. It wasn't that easy. First, the receptionist didn't want to hear the story. She wondered what the hell an old man was doing jumping up and down like a schoolgirl, trying to tell her he had powers." My cheeks got hot at the memory. "She finally got someone to come see me."

"Dr. Timson, this haughty bitch, actually brought a hero with her to protect her. I tried to tell her, to show her my power, and, well, she just told me she didn't allow powers from unregistered heroes in the Academy, and the brute hero actually put his hamhock of a hand on me to stop me. Like I can hurt her by taking off my leg."

"You can take it off?" Ian asked, eyes wide.

"Wanna see?"

He nodded. I stood up, still relishing the feel of standing on my own. I reached down to my right leg and grabbed it above the knee and gave it a quick twist. I hopped back a little to let it slide out of my pants leg. They stared at it, a bloodless severed leg, lying on the bar floor.

"That is so goddamn awesome," Ian said.

"Um, that is impressive, Barry, but how do I get rid of a severed leg?" Keepsie asked nervously.

"No problem there," I said. I got my right leg to grow back with a thought, and when it filled out to its right size, the one on the floor disappeared with a pop. I bent down and picked up the shoe and sock it had left behind and got back on the bar stool.

"That must have been quite a blow," Peter said quietly. "You finally got what you'd wanted your whole life, and suddenly no one cared."

"You said it. I wondered if Jack and Doodad and Seismic Stan had the right of it, trying to put those heroes in their place. I stomped out, looking for the first place to get a drink. And then I came here."

Keepsie winked at me and refilled my beer. "Location location location," she said. "Whatever the reason, Barry, we're glad to have you. You're welcome to drink here, you won't find many people here who aren't First or Third Wave powers. No heroes. And hero-lovers get a pretty good idea they're not welcome either."

"So what are your stories?" I asked.

Peter checked his watch. "There's no time for all three of us. I can identify people's emotions through their odors. Keepsie can, well, keep anything she owns. No one can take anything away from her, I mean. And Ian, well..." he paused, looking at the man next to him, who seemed to go from happy to glum like a summer storm.

"They wanted to call me 'Feculent Boy' in school, if that tells you anything," Ian said, grinning.

I shook my head. "I drive a bus for a living, kid. Don't really know what freculate means."

Keepsie laughed, but I could tell it wasn't at me. "Ian can shoot, to put it delicately, the contents of a toilet out of his fists. It's a powerful stream, I think he could have been a hero, as it's a pretty strong power, but the Academy thought it wasn't 'hero-like' to..."

"To shoot shit out of your hands," Ian finished for her. He didn't look upset, he'd seemed more mad about the surfing competition.

I sat for a moment. "Those have got to be good stories."

Peter patted me on the shoulder and threw some money on the bar. He stood, straightened his jacket, and waved to Keepsie. "I have to go, I have an early class to teach tomorrow. Barry, it was a pleasure to meet you, I hope we can talk more later. Ian, sorry about the surfing competition."

I shook his hand and he left.

"Another round?" I asked Ian, who grinned at me. I was willing to buy the good stuff this time.

I hadn't made it into the Academy. I hadn't gotten what I'd wanted my entire life. I'd never though that the First and Third

Wave powers would have the same thoughts about the heroes that I did.

The near-constant ache in my chest had lifted that morning, then tightened horribly when I was in the Academy, and now it was gone again. But I felt like part of something. Something super.

Mister Adventure and the Race Against Time

Davey Beauchamp

Mister Adventure winced as he touched the back of his head. The AtomiK Fist must have sucker punched him from behind, because there was no way he could have taken Alex in a fair fight. It took him a moment to gain his bearings because he wasn't in the last place he remembered being. And it didn't help that the blow to the back of the head was delivered by the AtomiK Fist's fist.

As Alex slowly rose to his feet, he felt like he was forgetting something very important. The fog in his mind still had yet to clear, but for the moment there were other pressing concerns. He began looking around and found himself once more, in what appeared to be a cell, something Alex (as Mister Adventure) was no stranger to.

Now all he had to do was wait for the villain, whom he figured was the AtomiK Fist, to enter, gloat and tell him his grand scheme. Alex was an old pro at this. And it seemed, so was his captor, since there was no furniture to speak of in the room. There was nothing in the room but himself to try and break down the door.

Alex walked over to the door, conscious of each step taken, to see if he might be able to see anything through the narrow slits in it. This was just your typical dungeonesque hallway, which kind of disappointed Alex. Since his time as Mister Adventure, he had seen such wonders and been held in some quite elaborate places.

Slowly Alex was starting to feel better and the freight train headache he was experiencing was down to truck, though for the life of him he knew that there was something missing. There was something Alex knew he was supposed to be doing, but he couldn't put his finger on it. In a way it was making him feel, on some level, helpless. It was a feeling he wasn't used to.

Mister Adventure looked down at his wristwatch and saw the time on it was going in reverse. He remembered when Dr. Richards gave all the League of Adventurous Heroes these special watches. It allowed them to keep track of time when they were truly racing against the clock. It had been an invaluable piece of equipment to them, but now he could not remember why it was set.

Alex just stared at the hands trying to unravel their hidden meaning as each tick led the hands of the watch backwards one more moment in time. The fog that was clouding his mind just wouldn't clear. Alex wondered if he had taken one too many blows to the head and it had finally caught up with him.

In the back of his mind, the fear of losing his mind and the ability to do what he did caused Alex to face his mortality once again, which led to the dark place that dwelled with in him. Where the rage and anger, which existed in all men, lived. Alex punched the wall as hard as he could, so he would feel something other than this looming dread that was growing within. It was followed by the sound of bones breaking.

It took a brief moment for the pain to register. First it had to travel up his fist into his arm, into his shoulder up his neck and then reached his brain. Alex took a breath, leaving his now broken fist pressed against the wall.

As the pain hit him he continued to look at his watch. His arm trembled as the pain coursed through his body. But in that pain it also gave Alex a moment of clarity. He knew once he was out of this cell and he stopped whatever evil scheme was taking place (and he would stop it) he would have to see Stephen to fix his hand. And that triggered the memories of why the watch on his wrist was counting down.

Alex dropped to his knees as the memories resurged.

Alex—no, *Mister Adventure*—recalled getting the phone call from the Sapphire City General Hospital in urgent need of his assistance. It seemed a young girl by the name of Susan needed an experimental drug known as penicillin to save her life-and time wasn't a luxury she had. This new drug in time had the potential to save many lives (including the fighting forces overseas) and not just Susan's. Penicillin had caught the attention of those who thrived in the wretchedness of villainy and scum, who now wanted this wonder drug for themselves so they could place it in the hands of the highest bidder.

His memories grew fuzzy again.

Alex remembered going to Chicago.

A man in a white coat handing him a box. A small box.

The memories and recalling them began to hurt.

The Sapphire City's skyline glowed in the sunset.

An explosion.

Climbing out of smoking remnants of a truck.

It was hot and hard to see.

Coughing.

"How do you like my new and improved *AtomiK punch!*"

Laughter!

Fighting.

Pain.

Heat.

Sweat.

Pain.

Laughter.

Darkness.

Then there was the cell.

Alex's face was blank, totally devoid of any sense of life or emotion. Then something inside just clicked-or better said snapped-as the countdown on his watch gave him less than an hour to find the penicillin and save Susan's life.

Taking over, Mister Adventure rose to his feet. He knew there was only one way out of that cell and it was through the door. The only battering ram he had was himself.

With all the speed and strength Mister Adventure could muster, he charged the door.

The sound of body intersecting with door rang forth over and over again. It was followed by the sounds of pain, bruising bones, and splintering wood. Then, without warning and to the point of Mister Adventure almost breaking himself, the door gave way under the assault.

Mister Adventure collapsed on the other side of the doorway. It took him a moment to work past the pain, which was now consuming him. The only thing keeping him going was the little girl in dire need of his help, as there was no way he was going to let her down.

Alex returned and rose to his feet and quickly discovered his right arm and shoulder were of no use. He took the remnants of his shirt and fashioned a sling to help alleviate some of the pain. After that Alex staggered down the hallway seeking the medicine and a way out.

After some time trying to navigate through the maze like corridors of his captor's abode, Alex came upon what appeared to be a grand dining or meeting hall and it was decorated to fit the bill out of a horror pulp.

Clapping filled the hall and Alex's attention was drawn to the head of the table. He could have sworn a moment ago no one was sitting there. Alex shook his head trying to work past the mind numbing pain that was consuming him.

It took him a few seconds to focus his eyes at the form sitting there.

Rage.

It began to consume Alex.

Under his breath and in barbaric fashion he called out the name of the man who sat before him, "Zhou!" A man who was single-handedly Mister Adventure's greatest nemesis. Dr. Zhou was an Oriental genius and underworld warlord who was bent on world domination and making Sapphire City his throne to rule from.

Alex wanted to charge Zhou, but there was no way he could. He just didn't have any fight left him. What little he did have was what was keeping him going to save Susan, though he had no idea where the penicillin was.

"Ah Mister Adventure," Zhou said in that thick oriental accent of his, "it is, a pleasure for *you* that you finally join us."

"I don't have time for this game;" Alex said angrily, "a little girl's life is at stake here."

Zhou just paused, looking at the war-torn Mister Adventure who stood before him. A lesser man would have let defeat overcome him—and that was what made Mister Adventure a worthy opponent.

"Mister Adventure, do not think I am the monster you truly believe I am," Zhou said, taking a small box out of the green silk haori he wore, "I believe this what you are looking for." Zhou placed the box on the table and slid it to the other end.

Alex's eyes widened as he watched the box slide across the table in horror, just knowing the fragile contents it held within would shatter if it fell upon the floor.

But the box stopped just short of the edge. Alex let out an unnoticeable sigh of relief.

"I had warned all in my employ not to interfere with the delivery of the penicillin," Zhou said very honestly, "and the AtomiK Fist has been dealt with. What can I say? Good help isn't an easy thing to find these days. Everyone wants to be the man who killed Mister Adventure, though the *honor* will go to me."

Alex didn't say a word. Frankly he had no idea what was going on, because he had never seen this odd benevolent side to Zhou before.

Zhou hit a button hidden beneath the table and a hallway, which Alex had not seen before, illuminated.

"Take the box and follow the illuminated path," Zhou said with a crooked smile. "It will lead you out of here. If you stray from the path let those consequences fall upon your head."

Alex just stared at Zhou.

"Go now before it is too late," Zhou said stroking his goatee in true villain fashion, "or before I change my mind."

Alex nodded his head in agreement. He made his way to the table as fast as he could and grabbed the box, making sure before he left that the contents of the box were still there and intact. Alex headed down the illuminated hallway and never once looked back.

Alex came out upon a street in the heart of Sapphire City, the city of tomorrow, today.

He looked down at his watch, only to see with horror that time had run out. And Alex had no idea how long it had been since that had happened. Any other man would have given up, but he was Mister Adventure, the man who would never give up. It didn't hurt that he was a man who believed in miracles.

The sights and sounds of the city began to overtake Alex as he tried with all of his might to move under the force of his own power towards Sapphire City General Hospital. The pain was too much for him, though, and he started blacking in and out of consciousness. People gathered around and at the same time moved away from the staggering Mister Adventure. They were not sure what to do.

Somewhere in the darkness of the confusion and pain in Alex's mind a sliver of reason shone. He saw a taxi and managed to climb in. And just as his body gave out on him Alex was able to tell the cabbie his destination.

The taxi flew down the streets of Sapphire City.

Alex shot up in the bed in which he was lying in sort of panic. Not knowing where he was or when, his mind was racing trying to put everything in order. Out of the corner of his eye he saw a form leaving the room through a door, and in a hurry. He heard what he thought was someone yelling *"doctor."*

Alex began to wonder if he had made it in time and the more he looked around it did appear he was in a hospital room. Then it hit him and he hurriedly touched his face making sure his mask was there, and it was.

He was sore but was feeling better. The pain had died. His eyes came to rest on the watch and the countdown counter resting at zero hour. Alex's spirit was crushed, because he knew in his heart there was no way he had saved Susan. He gripped the sheets hard as a tear welled up in his eye that would never escape the mask he wore.

Alex fell back into the bed and stared up at the ceiling trying not to the let the grief he was feeling get the better of him.

The door to the hospital room opened and it sounded like several individuals entered but Alex didn't respond-he just kept staring up at the ceiling. Alex wasn't sure how he would act when he was told Susan had died, due to his failure.

Voices began to fill the room, but Alex only heard noise.

Then a single voice cut through the noise-the voice of a child! Alex rose in the bed and all in the room grew silent. His eyes must have been playing a trick on him because that was Susan and she was alive, but there was no way it could be her. Or maybe he had died from his injuries and this was not real, because how many people could cheat death as many times as he had without it finally catching up with him.

"Your plan was a success," a balding doctor with wire rimmed glasses proclaimed with excitement. He looked somewhat familiar to Alex, but he couldn't put two and two together. His head and memories were still a mess from his ordeal with AtomiK Fist at the city limits.

"They went after you just like you expected, allowing the real courier to deliver the medicine safely," the doctor said with a smile, "so we could save Susan and, in time, countless others."

Alex was at a loss for words, but Alex and Mister Adventure shared a smile, knowing this time he had been lucky and because of it a little girl's life was saved.

About the Contributors

Robert J. Sawyer has been called "the dean of Canadian science fiction" by The Ottawa Citizen, and has written 17 novels, including *Frameshift, Calculating God, Flashforward,* and his most recent novel, *Rollback.* Sawyer has won every major SF award, including the Hugo, the Nebula, and nine Canadian Science Fiction and Fantasy Awards (Auroras). He lives just west of Toronto with his wife, the poet Carolyn Clink.

Mike Resnick is a prolific, award-winning author and editor. His many novels include *Kirinyaga, The Widomaker, The Widowmaker Reborn,* and others too numerous to mention. He has won the Hugo, the Nebula, Asimov's Reader's Poll, the Japanese Seiun, and many other awards for his fiction.

Cory Doctorow is a writer, activist, speaker, and blogger. He is the author of the novels *Down and Out in the Magic Kingdom, Eastern Standard Tribe, Someone Comes to Town, Someone Leaves Town,* and the collections *A Place So Foreign* and *Eight More* and *Overclocked: Stories of the Future Present,* as well as co-author of the nonfiction book *The Complete Idiot's Guide to Publishing Science Fiction,* with Karl Schroeder. Cory is a frequent contributor to *The New York Times, Wired, MAKE,* and *Popular Science.*

Ernest Hogan is the author of the novels *High Aztec, Cortez on Jupiter,* and *Smoking Mirror Blues,* as well as several short stories for magazines such as *Science Fiction Age, Asimov's, Amazing Stories, Last Wave, New Pathways, The Red Dog Journal, Proud Flesh,* and the anthologies *Witpunk, Angel Body and Other Magic for the Soul,* and *Semiotex(e) SF.*

Lucy A. Snyder has sold over 70 short stories, 20 poems, and so much nonfiction she has lost count. She is author of the collections *Sparks and Shadows* and *Installing Linux on a Dead Badger (and Other*

Oddities). She lives in Ohio with her husband, author Gary A. Braunbeck.

James Palmer has written articles, interviews, reviews, columns, and poetry for *Strange Horizons, The Internet Review of Science Fiction, SciFaikuest, Continuum Science Fiction, Tangent, RevolutionSF,* and *Blood Blade and Thruster: The Magazine of Speculative Fiction and Satire.* He is a freelance copywriter and business journalist, and lives in Georgia with his wife Kelley and one very spoiled Chihuahua.

Gary A. Braunbeck has won the International Horror Guild and Bram Stoker Awards for his fiction. He is author of the novels *Prodigal Blues, Keepers* and the nonfiction book *Fear in a Handful of Dust: Horror As a Way of Life,* as well as many other novels and stories. He lives in Ohio with his wife, author Lucy A. Snyder.

Eugie Foster lives in a slightly haunted, mildly fey-infested home in Metro Atlanta with her husband Matthew and skunk Hobkin. She received the 2002 Phobos Award for her short story "All in My Mind", and her work has been nominated for the British Fantasy, Bram Stoker, Southeastern Science Fiction, Parsec, and Pushcart awards. Eugie is also the managing editor of *Tangent.*

Mur Lafferty is a freelance writer, podcaster, and mom. She is author of the books *Lessons from a Geek Fu Master* and co-author of *Tricks of the Podcasting Masters,* and has sold fiction to *Escape Pod* and several other publications. Mur produces and hosts the popular podcasts *Geek Fu Action Grip* and *I Should Be Writing,* and is currently searching for an agent for her first novel.

Davey Beauchamp is the author of the *Agency 32* series and creator of *The Amazing Pulp Adventures Radio Show Starring Mister Adventure.* He is the editor of two popular *Writers for Relief* anthologies, which raise money for survivors of hurricanes Katrina and Rita. He was recently hired to write a rock opera based on the fairy tale of Bluebeard. He lives in North Carolina, where he works as a computer tech and YA librarian.

www.ingramcontent.com/pod-product-compliance
Lightning Source LLC
Chambersburg PA
CBHW031837170626
46807CB00004B/1504